CW01510857

Broken Instruments

Broken Instruments

Recollections of a Luthier

WILLIAM VARNAM

© William Varnam, 2021

Published by Broken Instruments Ltd

A CIP catalogue record for this book is available from the British Library.

ISBN 978-1-5262-0921-4

Book layout and cover design by Clare Brayshaw

Drawings by William Varnam

Prepared and printed by:

York Publishing Services Ltd
64 Hallfield Road
Layerthorpe
York YO31 7ZQ

Tel: 01904 431213

Website: www.yps-publishing.co.uk

"Broken instruments
Can be mended, then
They will play again once more
And the song once lost
Somewhere way back when
Will return to you for sure."

Phil Baggaley

"A violin should be played with love or not at all."

Joseph Wechsberg

Contents

Introduction

It was the book "Violins of Hope" by Dr James A Grymes that became the catalyst for the writing of a musical dramatization called "Broken Instruments". Dr Grymes tells the true story of how real-life Luthier Amnon Weinstein came to devote his skills and time to the restoration of violins that were once played by incarcerated Jews during the Holocaust.

At least for a few of these persecuted Jews, life in a concentration camp could become a little more tolerable if you were fortunate enough to play an instrument, and in particular, the violin. Playing an instrument meant that you could perform for the pleasure of your persecutors, and in return improve your chances of survival by receiving better food, and at least some improvements to your living conditions.

The various moving stories of rescued violins that came into the hands of Amnon inspired musician and songwriter, Phil Baggaley, to write a song titled "Broken Instruments". His listeners rapidly became aware that this song was saying something rather special, and Phil soon came to realise that the song had a life beyond the pages of the music and the studio microphone. This was when he contacted me with an invitation to collaborate with him to produce a script telling the story of a fictitious character who we called Ari Vander. Phil and I have worked together on various theatrical projects over recent years. Like Amnon, Ari is a Luthier. The difference between these two Luthiers is that Ari, in our story, is a Holocaust survivor who experienced the life-saving powers of the violin and who in later life also devoted his skills and time to the restoration of Holocaust instruments.

The unexpected cloud of Covid-19 quickly put an end to our plans to rehearse and stage the resulting musical dramatization, but the cloud lifted a little, when we managed to get a team of talented individuals together to produce "Broken Instruments" as an audio version. At the time of writing this introduction, the audio play has not yet been launched into the airwaves but you, dear reader, may by now have listened to it, if our efforts to get it on the airwaves have been successful. If you have experienced the audio version of this story, you will also have heard the touching songs crafted by Phil Baggaley and beautifully orchestrated by another talent named Mark Edwards. The equally adept Daniel Ellis directed a host of accomplished actors and did much technical wizardry. Rob Bullock was at the helm at the recording desk

It is Phil Baggaley and Dr Grymes who I must thank right now for their inspirational influences. This is a work of fiction, but which has its foundations firmly fixed in true events. And now, on with the story told through the recollections of Ari Vander from his workshop in 1980.

Broken Instruments

An account from the memory of Ari Vander

Here follows my personal account concerning the power of music. Music has many powers and many origins. It belongs to no one, because it belongs to us all, whoever we are and wherever we are from. It is the common language of humankind. It is always willing to speak to us. It asks nothing except that we listen. The rest is up to us.

I write this account in a much more modern world than the one I was brought up in; a world that never ceases to unfold its mysteries and marvels. I write at a time when, in just the previous year, Jupiter's rings were revealed in full photographic glory from the lens of Voyager 1; an unmanned craft which carried messages from humanity to the Cosmos. These messages included greetings in fifty-five languages. One of them was the recording of young boy saying, 'Greetings from the children of planet Earth.' Another included the first two bars of

Beethoven's String Quartet number 13 in B flat. I wonder what he would have made of it.

I could, it has to be said, have offered you even more global landmarks from the year 1979 but this is now 1980, and it is time for me to evoke images, and represent events of a different kind, which I will attempt to reproduce through the lens of my memory; landmark events that happened on planet Earth in my formative years. Events which shook it to its core.

I like to think that my narrative will also have some messages. If it does, then I sincerely hope that they will be messages from which all humanity can benefit. Like Voyager 1, the words of a young boy are featured in these writings. This is a young boy, who was incredibly fortunate to have been allowed to grow into a man. Come to think of it, even Beethoven gets a mention, albeit a brief one.

I place my various recollections in chapters for easy reference, as one would when writing a book. Should these recollections ever be published, then I should be more than happy for them to be called a book, and even happier if the reader felt that they had learned something from it, and that ultimately, what they learned was for the good of humankind. For books, like music, are always willing to speak to us. A book asks nothing except to be read. The rest is up to us.

'As a Luthier I have many instruments in my possession and in my care.'

Chapter 1

My Workshop and Residents

I consider myself to be in reasonable condition considering my past experiences. I do not particularly like to dwell on my past, and yet I suppose I should thank it for shaping me and making me what I am today, a survivor. A survivor yes, but from what, you may ask. I have heard many people say that they have survived what life has thrown at them. In my case, it seems more appropriate to say that I have survived what death has thrown at me. You see, I live, and there are far too many who I have known and shared common experiences with who, right now, do not live and who have perhaps been forgotten. Yes, I live. Ari Vander lives. Seventy years of age and born in a small medieval village in the Hessen region of central western Germany, but now living and working in Tel Aviv, Israel. Back then, when I sojourned with death, I was a musician who had also been trained by his father to make beautiful violins. It was playing a violin that saved my life, and knowing how to make and repair them, has sustained me in my later years.

Oh, forgive me. I said that I did not particularly like to dwell on the past, yet here I am waxing lyrical about it. I could never apologise however, for wanting to keep a certain story alive, and for wanting to dedicate whatever skill and energy I have left in my ageing body, into breathing new life into instruments that once played in the concert halls of death and destruction. So, let me continue my reminiscences, and let them express not only sorrow and despair, but also happiness and hope.

As a Luthier I have many instruments in my possession and in my care, but the most precious to me are the violins. People often ask, 'How should a good violin sound?' There is only one reply to such a question, 'It depends on the player.' There is no denying it is a hard instrument to learn and yes, it can be painful to the ears. But in the right hands! Oh, in the right hands is it not the nearest thing you have ever heard to the human voice?

Indeed, it is this unique quality that violin makers strive to re-create, after all, they are almost human – the violins that is – you can make up your own mind about Luthiers. Violins have a body do they not, ribs, and even a belly. Hearing me talk about them in this way, you could be forgiven for thinking that I look upon them as my family. Well, I do. And like all families, they can become quite demanding. You know, it can take two hundred and fifty hours to make a violin, and a complete restoration can take up to eighteen months. Long hours. Very, long hours. Hours of love. And when I think about violins, I experience love. I dwell in it. You see, I like to think that the relationship I have with my violins is allied to that of a dedicated parent to their children. And why not, there was a time when this instrument became my greatest ally.

My, oh my. Time has indeed flown. As I write this, I can hear the distant bells of the clock tower in the square adjacent to my workshop. Like my instruments, they speak to me. They tell me it is time to put away my tools, tidy the workbench, sweep the floor, and see to it that my children get safely to bed. This is the ritual to which I have become fondly attached. I bid them all goodnight and invite them to sleep well, and to rest assured that I shall see them all tomorrow. You have no idea how reassuring it is for me to be able to say, even to an imagined family, that I shall see them all in the morning.

I give them names, the origins of which you will discover later in my narrative. I imagine them launching into impish behaviour when I have left the room, being playful and full of joy. And with this belief, I gently warn them to behave in my absence. I comfortingly remind

Mendel that when I return, he shall have new strings. Mordechai shall have his purfling attended to, and I tell him that this should not be an embarrassment, for it can happen to the best of us. Finally, Yochanan is dutifully informed that, in the morning, his dislodged soundpost will be a mere formality to put right.

You have by now, I expect, grown to realise that these instruments mean a great deal to me. More than just the materials from which they were made. I cannot help myself. If you could only see them as I can. They hang here on the workshop wall, in their rows, and no doubt, to the untrained eye, they must look incredibly similar, silent for the moment and patiently waiting for attention. But in the arms of a good player, they each have their own personality, their own sound. No two violins are the same you know, but they are all full of music. And as well as music, I must add something further to their endearing qualities; they must also be full of wisdom. Why do I say this? Because my friend, (I do hope I can use this term to describe you dear reader), the violin has given birth to many a wise word. My teacher once told me:

'Ari, when you play the violin, you are somebody. And remember, a violin should be played with love or not at all. Learn the violin and it will teach you to forgive.'

At the time of course, I didn't fully understand what my teacher meant by all this, and it was some years later before I was, enlightened, shall we say? Subsequently, I did grow wiser and, if I may, I should like to share some of this wisdom with you. It is this; never itemise anything by number; always assign it a name. Secondly, never select anything. Instead, choose it. I would never, under any circumstances, wish to be selected for anything. Thirdly, in the Synagogue, in the theatre, the concert hall, the cinema and even at home, never sit on the right. And finally, never stand on a train. If you cannot find a seat, alight, and wait for the next one. Do these maxims sound like riddles? Perhaps so, but I can assure you that their origins and meaning reside within these writings.

And now, surely you must be asking yourself, 'What kind of man is this? Who is this Ari Vander the Luthier, and what could possibly have happened in his life to make him so passionate about violins?' Well, my friend, it all began at a wedding.

'… in moments, the place was a sea of sound
and motion …'

Chapter 2

At the Wedding

I have heard people describe weddings. I have heard them marvel at the size and grandeur of the venue and listened to the delight in their voices as they recalled the people they met and what they wore. You must appreciate, my friend, that a boy of ten by the name of Ari Vander, would have paid little attention to such things, but he did remember that the scene of his first ever wedding was an intoxicating mixture of movement, solemnity, and joy. There are many rituals associated with a Jewish wedding ceremony. By tradition, the bride and groom refrain from seeing one another for one week before that great event which unites them. On the day, there are contracts to be signed, after which the parents of bride and groom break a plate. Then there is the veiling ritual. And who could fail to be impressed by that wonderful moment when the bride and groom enter the ceremonial room like royalty. They are escorted towards the rabbi beneath a chuppah, a kind of canopy, which is supported by four poles carried each by a significant person. And then there are the numerous blessings and other goings-on.

What was a small boy to make of all this fuss and flamboyance? That small boy, I can tell you, was in awe of everything, even though he understood little about all the goings-on. Yes, I really was. My eyes were everywhere. My mother, however, was much more in tune with things and she wasn't going to miss an opportunity to put me in the picture. The sound of her kind but authoritative voice prompted me to focus my attention.

'Look, Ari, you'll miss it. See the bride and groom beneath the chuppah? Watch and listen.'

And there they were, just like mother said, standing beneath this carefully improvised canopy. To me it looked like a prayer shawl connected to a pole at each corner and then held aloft (I later discovered it was indeed a prayer shawl). Standing in front of the bride and groom was the rabbi. I have to say that I was completely puzzled by his actions. He placed a perfectly good wine glass inside a cloth bag and carefully set it beneath one of the groom's feet, whereupon the groom then proceeded to stamp on it and completely shatter the glass. The entire room instantly exploded into shouts of, 'Mazel Tov.' So alarmed was I at this, that I tried to hide behind my mother, but it seemed that we were surrounded. I felt in need of protection, or at least some words of reassurance that a riot wasn't going to break out. It was fortunate for me, that my mother was a living encyclopaedia of Jewish wisdom. Slightly afraid I might have been, but fear did not extinguish my desire to know more. What was all this Mazel Tov business? What did it mean? Mother was quick to read my thoughts and deliver an answer.

'Ari, I can see you are wearing that enquiring look. Ever the inquisitive boy. Let me explain. The word Mazel literally means a drip from above.'

At this, I simply started looking up at the ceiling expecting to discover a leak, but before I could question her further, she directed me to look at the rabbi, and to keep quiet for a moment. This man was obviously important, and he was about to speak.

'As the breaking of the glass reminds us that even at the height of personal joy, we must also remember the destruction of Jerusalem, so too must we remember the deep mystical connection between wine and marriage. It is said that wine gladdens the heart. But in order to produce this heart-gladdening liquid, the grape must first be crushed. Life is full of crushing moments. The key is to overcome these moments together and to find new levels of love and happiness. May this drip of inspiration from your soul above not dissipate, but rather have a positive and lasting effect, that from this event onwards you should live your life with higher consciousness. Be aware of the blessings in your life and be ready to receive more and more.'

No sooner had the rabbi finished speaking, the whole building shook to the reverberating shouts of 'Mazel Tov' followed by 'Siman Tov' and then a joyous chorus of 'Yehe Lanu' broke out and in moments, the place was a sea of sound and motion as they danced the hora.

And thus, I learned that these exclamations and what, at one point in the proceedings could only be described as acrobatics, was the way in which good wishes and congratulations were expressed at a Jewish wedding. Prior to this knowledge, this young impressionable boy thought he was watching a bunch of people jumping up and down and shouting something about how good it is to have a leaking roof. But my friend, despite being just a little afraid and not a little confused, on that day, good fortune must have poured down upon me, for it was then that I began to fall in love.

Of course, at the time, I would not have known that I was experiencing love, but something was stirring deep inside. It was a happy feeling, a good feeling. And yet, this was a different kind of happiness and a different kind of goodness. I had heard people talk about strange uncontrollable forces that could suddenly overcome a person. They had called it love, so this must have been just that. But the passion that had been released in me on that day was mostly for the music and, especially for one particular instrument. Had my father been with us, he would have been pleased, and no doubt relieved, to at last see me showing an interest in the very thing that had earned him a fine reputation, and a reasonable living. The voice of the violin had entered my soul. But wait! Did I say that the passion released in me that day was mostly for the music? There is more to tell. I was not the only one in the room to be affected in such a way. A girl, young like me, was standing and craning her neck to see over the shoulders of the elders. She too was captivated. Her gaze was fixed in the direction of the musicians. Momentarily, she turned her head and our eyes met. As quickly as it happened, we both looked away.

That was it. A fleeting glance. At the time, it was so quick that I would have had difficulty in explaining to anyone exactly what she looked like, except to say that her head was adorned with flowers. But believe me, in that moment I experienced something that I can only describe as, well, an aura; a feeling I had never felt before.

The music had entered my soul but this girl, whoever she was, had entered my heart. I later discovered that her name was Rose. Yes, on that day, I really had fallen in love.

"The violin or so they say
Can sound just like the human voice
And in some way, I can't explain
Can somehow play your heart strings
Make sense of these things
And feel your pain."

*'… only to receive the biggest kick up my backside
propelling me headlong …'*

Chapter 3

A Quest for Love

What does a young boy do? The violin had entered his very soul and a mysterious young girl had stolen his heart. Heart and soul cannot live separately; they must be together. I needed a plan. It struck me that if she too was attracted to the violin, then surely the violin held the key to our togetherness. This realisation made me leap with joy, and it became impossible for me to contain myself. I called out, 'Halevai' which of course means if only, I hope so, I wish. And I did hope and wish.

Now, as any child will know, a parent cannot teach them anything. At least, that's how it seemed to me, at the age of ten. It therefore came to pass that I was able to insist upon taking violin lessons from Mr Spielman. How could my father refuse? We both knew where my future lay. Despite being quite advanced in years, Mr Spielman had an excellent reputation, and his house studio was within reasonable walking distance. Alas, my beginnings under his tuition were somewhat frustrating for me.

Oh, those lessons. Lesson one: how to hold the bow; lesson two; how to hold the violin; lesson three; notation on the open strings; lesson four, playing posture. All of which I knew. My father had made sure of that. But Mr Spielman insisted I followed his methods. Easier said than done. Poor Mr Spielman. I can hear him now.

'Ari, you want to play the violin very badly, don't you?'

Naturally, I told him that indeed I did.

'And you will Ari. And you will. You will learn to play the violin extremely badly if you do not pay attention to what I am telling you!'

No disrespect to Mr Spielman, but I had a sense of urgency. I had a mission to complete, and I needed inspiration. Sure enough, inspiration came. It came in answering the call of nature. But not in the way you might be thinking. I had heard that birdsong had inspired music for centuries, and birds had a good-sized repertoire. My next step was obvious. I had to take to the woods.

And so began my quest, to learn how to imitate beautiful birdsong on my beginner's violin. I can hear it now, that moment in the first movement of Gustav Mahler's second symphony; the sound of the cuckoo. Oh, how well I mastered those two sublime notes. Who could fail to be impressed by my artistry? I played those notes over and over and over again, even at the risk of sending my violin teacher into an induced coma. First the 'cuc' and then the 'koo' and then together. 'Cuckoo.' In the woods I played, in the fields I played, and in the streets of my village I played. Oh, how I played.

On one singularly memorable occasion, I started to play beneath the open window of a house I was passing. To my delight, someone threw a coin in my direction. I carefully placed my instrument on the nearby window ledge in order to search for my reward. There it was. I bent over to pick it up only to receive the biggest kick up my backside propelling me headlong with such force, that only a thick oak door stood between me and perpetual motion. Door and head collided to a sound which made a very passible impersonation of distant cannon fire. So outraged was I, that I spun around to chastise my assailant, striking the door with a fist as I did so. Suddenly, the door behind me opened. I heard the latch. In a posture reminiscent of Victor Hugo's Hunchback of Notre-Dame, I turned to see who had opened it. No dear friend, it was not Esmeralda. It was the girl who had stolen my heart. I had obviously made quite an impression, but not of the kind I would have hoped to make. There was only one thing to do. I ran.

I ran from my embarrassment, ran from my indignation, ran the entire length of the village, and with bursting lungs, I begged the neighbouring woods to swallow me up. With my face buried in the green carpet beneath the trees, I steeled myself not to cry. There are times, in a young boy's life, when he needs to be by himself. It wasn't long, however, before I discovered that I was not alone. There came in the distance, a man's voice.

'Come comrades. Put your heart into it. Now, two three and.'

In perfect timing with the rhythm of the man's counting, music burst forth as if the very woods were ablaze with it. Joyous, happy music. Another wedding? Surely not, and besides, only Ari plays in the woods. It appeared that I had a rival or rather several of them. I closed my eyes and listened for a while. This action, however, proved to be a mistake. Having only just recovered from the embarrassment of receiving a good kick up my backside, I suddenly found myself being dragged to my feet by a strong hand which had grabbed the back of my collar. The move was punctuated by a gruff call.

'Ha! Got you!'

I struggled, but it was no use. The man called out to a group of people in the near distance, now easy to distinguish in their bright clothing against the green hues of the trees and vegetation.

'It seems we have a spy in the camp, comrades.'

A second voice responded.

'Is he armed?'

At this there was a roar of laughter. I managed to swing my head around, for it had been virtually buried in my captor's coat flaps. Truly, this scene was even more colourful than the wedding I had recently attended, but at this moment in time I was even more frightened and confused. I sensed hostility towards me and there was no mother to protect me. I steeled myself a second time. This was certainly no time to cry or show any signs of fear. Well, maybe just a little fear in this case. The man who had got me in his grip seemed to be the leader, and he had much to say for himself. As he gave answer to his comrade's question, he manoeuvred me like a puppet into the centre of their encampment.

'Armed you ask, Besnick. I would raise the question with him, but it seems rude as we have not yet been introduced.' The man pushed me clear of his bulky frame, whereupon he took a bow as if humbling himself before me. 'I am Nicu' he continued, 'and in case you are wondering, I have the pleasure of leading this Romani Troupe which you have chosen to invade. Now, who do I have the honour of addressing?' He grabbed my collar again. 'What is your name boy?'

'If you please sir, Ari.' I said as bravely and as meekly as I could.

'You hear that comrades. The boy has manners!'

This was just the opportunity for one of the others to join in the entertainment. I later learned that his name was Zindello.

'Oh, such a shame, Nicu. I was hoping to have to teach him some.'

It was now the turn of one of the women to contribute. 'Speak up boy. It sounds to me that you are ashamed of your name.'

At this, Zindello raised a hand. 'Nadya speaks the truth,' he declared, which instantly received a collective response and they all cried, 'The truth!' After which, they all spat. Fortunately for me they aimed at the ground.

Another Romani called Besnik now came forward. 'Your appearance gives you away boy. You of all people should know that a Jewish name is the keystone of your identity. For you are Jewish? Is that not the truth?'

The troupe were now stirring, and all, once again, hailed it to be 'The truth' following up with another collective spit.

Besnik continued, 'Your name, Ari, is who you are. And more; it is a channel for your spiritual energy.' He turned towards his peers. 'Do I not speak the truth?'

There was yet another collective 'The Truth' followed by the spitting, which was the signal for their leader Nicu to intervene.

'Enough! Too much talk and not enough music. I see you have not come alone. Look Nadya, he holds a violin to his breast as if it were an infant child. Do you play, boy?'

At last, I thought. Here was an opportunity to win these people over and to at least, earn my release from this worrying woodland encounter. 'Oh yes sir,' I replied, 'I have been practising every day.'

Nicu finally released his grip and bellowed out, 'Then let us waste no more time. Come, play for us little man.' He then called Zindelo into action. 'Zindelo, make yourself useful. Our guest requires a stage worthy of his physical presence.'

Of course, what Nicu meant by this was down to the fact that I was so small, the troupe members could hardly see me. Zindelo sprang to his task, and within seconds I found myself being lifted onto a makeshift stage, fashioned from old wooden boxes, and packing cases. With a gesture of triumph he said, 'Here maestro, take the stage. Your audience awaits.'

This would be the third time that I had to steel myself on that day in the woods. I took a deep breath, and carefully placed my instrument between chin and shoulder. After a few tentative seconds of tuning, I held my bow aloft in preparation for the big moment. I knew my piece so well, that I closed my eyes as I lowered the bow to caress the strings. I played with gusto, and out came the sound of my well-rehearsed cuckoo composition. I gave them a generous five seconds' worth. But instead of being greeted with tumultuous applause, it was met with a chaotic outburst of very loud, uncontrollable laughter.

But I was not beaten. I held my ground and continued to play. I even opened my eyes as a gesture of defiance. It was an act, however, that was rewarded in the most unexpected way. Right there, in the middle of the woods, among the dapple shades of nature's leafy awning, there were flashes of red, yellow, and gold, as the entire Romani troupe erupted into dance. I could have been in fairyland. To this day I can close my eyes and see them all spinning and leaping, and I can hear their music, as they improvised around my cuckoo song and produced a mercurial Romany Rhapsody.

"I've heard it said that when you play
A part of heaven can come down
And through a melody just say
All we never could do
All you ever wanted to say to me."

'…my brother Levi and I, put on a good show
with our jazz quintette.'

Chapter 4

Gypsy Swing

There are times when I could wish myself back into that glorious gypsy garden. It was certainly a second significant experience of my youth. Life was unpacking itself in front of me, flinging out one experience after another. You have to be quick to catch them, these life experiences. They are like clothes being flung out of a trunk. I use this analogy, because for me, experiences are like garments. You see, we need clothes primarily for protection, whether that be from the cold or from harmful substances, or as part of our identity or profession. Do you notice that I have omitted to mention the wearing of clothes simply for the purpose of looking good? Believe me, I am one of those people who could never look good in anything. And besides, I feel the most comfortable, and the most protected, in my overalls and apron. But clothes as life experiences? Yes, for as I have already said, we need them, but sometimes they don't seem to fit properly, or they don't feel right. And maybe sometimes, we must put them to one side, and try something else.

Of course, unlike clothes, we cannot throw experiences away. They are always with us. And like my woodland experience, we can, from time to time, get them out and try them on. Whatever the passage of time, we can make them fit in our imaginations, and they feel good. Other experiences, we try to keep secured in that proverbial memory trunk. We don't want to unpack them; that is, until we start to write them down. Some may not be particularly bad or harmful, but they can trigger negative feelings like regret or embarrassment. I can recall many days from my boyhood and adolescence that hold somewhat embarrassing memories.

And so, I trust you will grant me licence to avoid giving any detail about the awkward moments of my youth, save to say that I gradually grew in confidence and skill as a luthier and as a musician. In my younger days, the suit of level headedness and responsibility seemed ill-fitting, but I was increasingly encouraged by loving and industrious parents to let my childhood go. Imitating birdsong in the woods and playing the violin beneath windows would not earn me a steady living and thus, under my father's guidance, my passion for making music was channelled into learning the art of violin making. Love making, in the old-fashioned sense of the word, would have to wait. Perhaps forever.

That day, when I stumbled upon the Romani encampment, proved to be a life changing experience. I found another passion. As if falling in love with the violin and a young girl had not been enough, I began listening to jazz. It's true to say that, finding jazz, became a most useful distraction for Ari Vander the young man. The young girl proved to be much more elusive. She seemed to disappear into thin air, but it was the airwaves that came to my rescue and lifted me clear of any imaginings of forming a relationship. I begged the use of a neighbour's radio to help quench my newly acquired thirst for swing. This American influenced style of music began to unfold its mysteries to me. The mystery of the girl, however, unfolded much later in my life. For the moment though, I was living in my jazz epoch.

Even in this, I found that I had competition. My younger brother Levi developed an even greater passion for what became known as gypsy swing, or gypsy jazz, as some called it. He was always the first to get to the radio. I never got around to asking him whether he had ever visited the woods ahead of me. I was more interested in orchestral music to begin with and would never have dared to mention jazz to Mr Spielman when I was under his wing. But as a young twenty something, who was still excited and curious from that Romani encounter, persuading my equally talented younger brother to form a five-piece ensemble, seemed an obvious thing to do. We needed an outlet, as young people do, and as I was the older brother, Levi graciously conceded to me owning the title of band leader. Levi was by then an accomplished violinist, as was I, but such was his enthusiasm for the music of the Quintette du Hot Club de France, that he laid down his violin and picked up the guitar.

This was in 1935 and I found myself living in a very different Germany than when I was a young innocent boy. As a boy, I took little interest in adult affairs as you can imagine, and, as a young man, I much preferred to talk about music than politics. Although I say it myself, my brother Levi and I put on a good show with our jazz quintette. The three who completed the line-up were very capable people, who we trusted on both a personal level, and as accomplished and committed musicians. We gained much confidence, in such a short space of time. We even had our own pre-rehearsed closing gambit which we repeatedly used to close our performances. I would do the honours. Here's how it went:

'Ladies and gentlemen, it has been our pleasure to perform for you all this evening. Time has got the better of us I'm afraid, but before we say our goodbyes, allow me to introduce you to the band; names you will no doubt recall in future years when you will say, I was there, that night, when the world knew not who they were, but it knows now.'

It was always the same. Firstly, I would introduce our double bass player Yaakov Schneider, then Asher Reichman on piano accordion, followed by Yosef Dorfman on guitar. Each in turn would play a short solo. I say short, but I don't think Asher, our accordion player, understood the meaning of the word. His solo was always somewhat stretched, shall we say, and he would positively glow when he received his applause. The rest of us glowed too, but more from restrained frustration and mild annoyance. After the three solos, I would then introduce my brother Levi, and he would dutifully deliver his own elaborate and skilful guitar solo. It was then Levi's turn to speak:

'And not forgetting ladies and gentlemen, on violin, my older brother and band leader, Ari Vander.'

We were not many years apart, but Levi always insisted upon introducing me as the older brother. I could hardly complain. After all, I had been allowed to call myself the band leader. In any case, I loved my brother, and I took this comment more as a compliment than an insult.

One engagement was particularly memorable, but not just for the amount of audience appreciation we received. The auditorium had cleared, and we were tidying up our music, and putting our instruments to bed for the night. Despite the fact that forming the quintette was my idea, at times, I felt that I had been letting Levi down a little, by not showing the same level of enthusiasm for it as he did. That is, I still embraced orchestral music, so my commitment to jazz, even though I loved it, was not exclusive. For me, this night's performance had been different though, and I was beginning to feel what I can only describe as the jazz heartbeat inside me. I wanted Levi to know this so, as we were putting the finishing touches to our careful packing away, and the stacking of our chairs, I served him a comment.

'We played well tonight, no?' I smiled and paused my activity waiting for his response.

'Well enough my brother. Well enough,' he replied rather dryly.

I was quick to express my surprise at this reply and said, 'Well enough? Did you not hear the applause, Levi? I tell you we are on to something with this new style of gypsy swing.'

'Swing is the right word, Ari. For if we get caught playing this forbidden music, we shall be the ones swinging.'

Again, I was quick in my attempt to turn this conversation into something positive. 'But you love this new music. Have you forgotten what you keep telling me? That this music is the future?'

It was clear to me by now that Levi was in no mood to exchange pleasantries. I could see bitterness in his eyes as he spoke.

'It is forbidden music here, Ari. Do you think we'd get a reception like we did tonight with just any audience? Was it not obvious, that the vast majority of our audience was Jewish? And brave Jews at that, to risk listening to the music of the American Southern States. Need I be any more explicit?' His voice now took on a sarcastic admonishing tone, 'How dare they fail to comply with the Chancellor's wishes and the rulings of the Reich Chamber of Music only to promote good German music. Is this courage, Ari, or foolishness?'

Of course, I knew that Levi was speaking the truth, but it had been such a wonderful evening. This Hamburg audience had opened its arms to us and I felt that I had to keep this alive. 'These restrictions will soon pass – '

Levi did not allow me to complete what I was about to say and burst in.

'Restrictions you call them! Laws, Ari. Laws! Have you needed a physician or a dentist recently? And when did you last see a Jewish police officer?'

I was determined to make light of these disturbing comments from my brother and offered, 'I hope never to see any kind of police officer. Hah! And I'm in no hurry to see a physician or a dentist.'

Levi began to contain himself a little at this saying, 'You are a good violinist, Ari. Yes, a very good violinist. Tell me, why did you decide to form this little gypsy jazz quintette of ours, eh? What was it that suddenly altered your appetite for serious music?'

Now it was my turn to be annoyed. 'What talk is this?'

'I'll tell you why, Ari. It was because no Jew can get a seat in the string section of any orchestra of merit. You know this, Ari. Restrictions!'

I struggled to save the situation and all I could manage was, 'But you love jazz, swing. That's why you put down your violin and picked up a guitar, which I might add, you play very well.'

Despite my efforts I could see that Levi was in no mind for reasoning or flattery. He had a determined look about him. There was no mistaking his position now. He told me plainly, that he would be playing more swing in the future, but before I could try to make some peace with him and assure him that the matter was therefore settled, his next comment shattered any illusions I had about him playing any future jazz with me. Levi was going to America.

Levi chased his declaration up with, 'As soon as I have the means.'

Once again, and in an increasing state of desperation and disbelief, I could only manage to say, 'Of course you will, Levi. Huh! You'll be the next Irving Berlin. Teach yourself piano like he did, and I'll come and see you in Tin Pan Alley! But not before our next rehearsal.'

Clearly this made no difference, and his final words as he walked out of the theatre were, 'I'll let the stage manager know you're still in the building.'

There came the firm hollow sound of a door closing and he was gone.

Despite being ever the optimist, I could not help but muse a little over what my brother had said to me that night, backstage, in Hamburg in 1935. I remember somehow not wanting to leave the theatre. There I sat on the one remaining chair that had somehow resisted being stacked. I didn't have the heart to unite it with the others. Then I heard the sound of footsteps approaching. I thought it must be the stage manager who would no doubt look at me admonishingly and point to his watch.

To my surprise, it was a most apologetic Yaakov, who told me that he could not make next week's rehearsal due to family business. The door had hardly closed behind him when an equally apologetic Asher appeared. Something about it being his birthday and he was sure I would understand. Huh! Since when did Asher celebrate his birthday? And then it was Yosef's turn. Apparently, they had all been discussing whether it made any sense to provoke the authorities, by continuing to play this forbidden music. They attempted to sweeten this remark by reminding me that they all had their families to consider, and that I was sure to understand.

It was Levi who had the last word. Even today, when I think back to that time, it reverberates inside my head. I should have been better prepared to hear it. The word was…America.

"From the ruins of a Synagogue
A Cantor's song is ringing out
For one day soon the truth will shout
They can take away our freedom
But they'll never break our spirits
No not this time."

'Give yourself a good start when you
get through that golden door.'

Chapter 5

America Calls

I knew that ocean liner travel was expensive, and that a good number of Jews had decided to travel alone, having been given the resources they needed from family members who must have made considerable financial sacrifices. I still wondered what all the fuss was about and resigned myself to believe that things weren't as bad as some people were making out. Perhaps this said more about how I saw myself in the grand scheme of things, and how I had accepted my given status, rather than the reality of the growing unrest that was beginning to permeate our communities.

For almost ninety years, since the middle of the nineteenth century, millions of Germans and Eastern Europeans had sailed from Hamburg to the New World. The Hamburg America Line carried emigrants across the Atlantic each year from the port of Cuxhaven on Germany's North Sea coast at the mouth of the Elbe River.

My stubborn condition of denial doggedly held me in its grip; a grip even more powerful than Nicu's, the Romani leader, who I had met in the woods as a boy. I could have done with his leadership at this time. He would have shaken me into action. My parents were even more resigned to their circumstances than I was, and they never discussed anything in my presence. It was as if they had just let go of everything they stood for; their values, their beliefs. They seemed so passive, and I completely failed to understand why. Yet, who was I to criticise their actions, or rather, lack of actions.

Cuxhaven would be busy, I told myself. It would be heaving with eager and nervous passengers. It would be full of strange sounds and comings and goings. It would be impossible to find Levi in time to say goodbye. Surely, he would understand. These words about understanding, had haunted me for the past year, when I had wrongfully resented the band for, as I saw it, deserting their duties in the quintette. I suppose I was the deserter of duties now. If this was my conscience speaking to me, then I am thankful for having one, and with absolutely no time to lose, I steeled myself once again to do the right thing.

Cuxhaven was indeed teeming with activity when I got there, but I was determined to let nothing get in my way. I had to see my brother and say a proper goodbye. I cannot say how I managed to get there, or even how I managed to get through to where the departures were taking place, such was my resolve and single-mindedness in completing my mission to intercept Levi. An impressive sight lay before me. Cranes swung cargo against the backdrop of the sky, and the air was filled with the sounds of voices giving instructions to direct awaiting passengers. All seemed confusion. Periodically the human hubbub would be drowned out by the deep, sonorous sound of a ship's horn, as though some angry leviathan had suddenly risen from the ocean depths; an ocean that separated the continents and which was about to separate whole families.

I could taste salt on my lips. My exertions in fighting my way through the crowds and keeping control of my own personal cargo, caused me to gulp in huge quantities of the damp sea air. I was in the open and yet I was beginning to feel claustrophobic. In my panic, I pushed even harder against the swell of living bodies and began calling out my brother's name in desperation. Finally, I saw him, already on the gangway to board the ship.

I hailed him once more, 'Levi! Levi Vander, Levi!'

At last my voice reached its target. My brother's sudden stop caused a human domino-like collision, and earned a few unrepeatable curses from some of the passengers, but he was too surprised and happy to see me to be aware of this.

'Ari!,' he called, 'had I known you were coming to see me off, I would have cleared the gangway. As you can see it's just a little busy here.'

Levi began to fight his way down to a better level from which to communicate with me. I realised that time was of the essence, so I came straight to the point.

'I have something for you.'

'No time, Ari. Seeing you is enough. I'll write. And don't worry big brother, I'll remember to say my daily prayers.'

A call came from one of the port officials, 'All aboard please! All aboard!' With no time to lose, I threw him one of the two pieces of cargo I was carrying.

'You'll pray better with this. Here! Make sure you catch it!'

Levi adeptly did so, saying, 'What is it?'

In the mid-1800s tens of thousands of Jews from German lands left their homes to make new lives in America. During this period, a miniature daily prayer book was printed in Germany. I had been in possession of a first of three editions. All I had to say to Levi was, 'Especially for travellers by sea to the nation of America,' for him to understand that he had just received a very precious book.

'How on earth did you come across a copy of this?' he marvelled.

With precious seconds ticking, there was no time for me to explain, other than to say, 'There's more.' I held out a larger and rather more delicate and even more valuable package. 'Here! Take this. You'll have to reach, brother, I'm not throwing this one.'

Levi realised what the second package was. 'No, Ari. I play guitar now. A violin is no use to me.'

I had to raise my voice now as the departure time came ever closer, and the crowds were even more eager to board the Atlantic-bound liner. 'Not for playing,' I shouted.

Levi gave a quizzical look and shouted back, 'How so!'

'A man must have means brother. When you get to America, sell it. It will take an experienced eye to find any damage. You'll still get a good price for it. Give yourself a good start when you get through that golden door.'

Levi's reply was one of friendly annoyance, 'I know what you are up to Ari Vander. This is the Amati isn't it? What kind of meshuggeneh notion is this? No! Ari. It was father's gift to you. Your inheritance, your birth right. No!'

I had made up my mind about this sacrifice and I would not be deterred. 'I'm past twenty-one now, Levi. I make my own decisions.'

Pleadingly Levi called back, 'No! Ari. No!'

Another boom of the ship's horn forced a pause until I said, 'If you don't take it, I swear I'll feed it into the mouth of the Elbe, and the river that takes you to the sea can keep it. Now, GO!'

*"How do you make your music
in the midst of all this hell?
Where darkness reigns beyond
belief and evil people dwell
How do you find relief for
just a moment in this place?
How do you find it deep inside
to plant one seed of grace?"*

'…and he will fall in the streets,
on the night of broken glass.'

Chapter 6

At Home and Abroad

Not that you would know, my reader friend, but I have had to take a little time away from writing up my story. I have been catapulted right back into 1980, with all the sights, sounds and smells of my workshop. A man must still earn a living you know. A living that I love, let me remind you. There is always another re-stringing task to perform, more purfling to address and another soundpost to put right. Tools have to be kept in tip top condition, and shavings have to be swept. Today, however, it was the task of answering the telephone which surprisingly gave me the greatest pleasure.

The telephone call was from the National Music Museum, University of Dakota. I could barely contain my joy at receiving the request to consider taking on the responsibility to restore an Amati. A genuine Amati would be a rare thing indeed and would date from the sixteenth century. Yes, an Amati was no stranger to me, just an old acquaintance. Andrea Amati introduced a characteristic amber coloured varnish to his instruments. To work on an Amati is a Luthier's dream. I had no need to consider this proposition. An Amati would be so rare and precious, that it was not likely to be played except in very special circumstances, and by a very special player. People would pay a great deal of money just to see one, let alone hear it.

Immediately I put the receiver down I had to put myself down; in a chair that is. I was almost dizzy from excitement. To think, an Amati, in my workshop, in my hands again; assuming the instrument turns out to be genuine of course. How could the thought of seeing and touching an Amati, not reach into the recesses of the heart? Who might have played it? How far would it have travelled to enchant the ears of audiences. And now I think of it, an Amati not only stimulates the blood supply. In my case, it stimulates the banks of the memory. Occupation is clearly a good remedy for painful memories. It shuts them out. Today, however, the barrier has been broken.

Why did it take my brother so long to write, after his Atlantic crossing? Call me a sentimental old fool if you like, but if you could see me now, you would witness me rummaging around frantically in one of my workshop drawers; a drawer that I reserve specifically for paperwork, such as invoices and receipts. Ah! Here it is. After such a long wait, I simply had to keep it; Levi's one and only letter to me; postmark 1938. Two years it took. I read it every now and again. It helps me to hear his voice once more. I shall read it to you now and you too can imagine my brother's voice.

'My dear brother,

Forgive me. I have been a little lacking in my enthusiasm when it comes to writing. But now things have had time to settle, I feel in a better position to send you some words of encouragement. I imagine that you must have often wished you had boarded that ship with me to sail towards that golden door. Have no regrets, dear brother. Celebrate. The German American press report very little of the affairs in Europe, and I can say that this is such a relief to me, knowing that, as you predicted, things did eventually settle down. No doubt you are enjoying playing your proper music back in the concert halls.

To be honest, Ari, many who took that Atlantic crossing have been expressing regret at leaving what we all considered to be our homeland. When we steamed into New York Harbour, we expected the Statue of Liberty to push open that golden door. Well, someone must have placed a blindfold over her eyes, because the door never really opened. Not without a struggle. Had she seen the faces of those hopeful destitute Jews, I'm sure she would have shed a tear.

As you know, Ari, many travelled alone, leaving their loved ones, such was the expense of sea-bound passage. It was a surprise to us that many American and German Jewish communities did not welcome us. You see, they were assimilated into the American way of life. Germany had no ties or connections for them. We immigrants, especially those who could only speak the German language, were seen as interlopers. Their inability to communicate went very much against them and they were looked upon as being arrogant and ungrateful. They became victims of hostility. Their accents and appearance are the subject of ridicule.

I suppose arriving on the shores of America at a time when the Great Depression was only just beginning to loosen its grip, wasn't good timing on our part. What did we know of their experience of unemployment, homelessness, and starvation? We all believed that we were heading for a better life when we boarded that steam ship. Which brings me back to that moment, my brother, when you stretched out your arms and placed that beautiful instrument into my hands.

Any success I have enjoyed in this country, Ari, lies with that violin and your selflessness. I promised myself that I would never sell it, but sell it, I did. And it saved my life, Ari. I shall never be able to repay you, but take comfort, in knowing that you will no doubt see brighter prospects for the future by staying where you are.

Your loving, and grateful brother, Levi.'

Even before that ship disappeared over the horizon, I had made up my mind that things would settle. After all, many of the German Jews had decided to stay. Why leave? They had demonstrated their patriotism during the so-called 'War to end all Wars'. Some had even been decorated. What had they to fear?

Yes, there were ever increasing restrictions, like, compulsory middle names for Jews. I became Ari Israel Vander and my passport had to be stamped with a letter J. This was to signify that I was a Jew. Policies, policies. Repressive? Of course. But primarily non-violent. That was important. Work was getting harder to find, but I was a good musician and so long as I was prepared to play good German music, and with so many vacant seats left by string players who had boarded those steam ships, there was always an opportunity for a concert violinist. Well, for a while at least.

And, believe me, some of those concerts were livelier than a Jewish wedding. The difference was, of course, that you never wanted the music to stop at a wedding, but after some concerts a musician would waste no time in exiting the building. We used to call it the post-finale-flee. In city streets, one could dodge danger. In a concert hall you were a captive target.

Speaking of targets, in the winter of 1938, Synagogues across Germany, from Bonn in the west, to Berlin in the east and from Hamburg in the north, to Munich in the south, burned. It would be heart-breaking to list them all. They were not the only buildings to be damaged as violence began to erupt throughout the late evening and early morning hours during the ninth and tenth of November. It became known as Kristallnacht and it marked the first instance under the regime we were now living, when Jews were incarcerated simply because they were Jews.

As I have indicated earlier in my narrative, I was more interested in reading music than reading publications on current affairs. Had I been more tuned in to the growing political unrest, I would have heard about the Polish Jewish boy of seventeen, who was aggrieved at his parents' expulsion from Germany along with thousands of others who had Polish citizenship, and who had been residing in Germany for many years. The boy went to the German Embassy in Paris where he was living at the time, and in an act of revenge, for his parents' imposed circumstances, he shot the diplomatic official who had been assigned to assist him.

It was coincidental that an important event in the National Socialist calendar was being marked at a commemoration in Munich. It transpired that certain individuals, with the power to do so, chose this occasion to make reply when they heard about the diplomat's assassination. He died two days after the shooting from his wounds. The Storm Troopers were mobilised.

And storm is exactly what they did, through the streets with voices full of fury, hearts full of hatred, and finally with blood on their hands. How could I have been so blinkered? How could they have been so cruel? The act of violence committed by the Storm Troopers forced many European Jews, and indeed the rest of the world, to finally begin to grasp just how ruthless this regime we were living in could truly be.

In the interests of dramatic effect, for which I offer no apology, let us imagine an individual unfortunate enough to be caught up in the mayhem. Perhaps he has just stepped outside from attending a concert, or perhaps he has been playing in an orchestra or jazz quintette. The hour is late, and our protagonist needs to breathe in a little night air. He must clear his head. He knows the town, or is it a city? He recognises the buildings and the various urban arteries. They are his familiar friends, and they will guide him safely home. Home, or so he believes, to a warm welcome.

Suddenly he hears a cry which stops him in his tracks. He listens and wonders who called out. He hears footsteps and recognises the quick light tread of a child, and the heavier scurry of an adult. Now come the voices of men, women, and of children, competing with the sounds of feet meeting the hard surfaces of slab, tile and stone. The footsteps hasten. Who is running? Who is chasing?

Why does this city not sleep at this late hour? Why do doors suddenly swing wildly open and windows break? Why do people flee, some bare-footed, some hardly clothed, and looking as if they have been literally dragged from their beds? They scatter. They run for their lives. Others lie motionless in the street.

Our invisible onlooker, with senses suddenly sharpened, hears voices which beg and plead. He sees their shadowy figures from a distance. Some give up begging and pleading and just sink to their knees. Other dark animated figures fling limp, lifeless forms into gravity's embrace. They hit the ground and add blood to the meandering thoroughfares. Blood flows like a viscous river. Red, like the flames that now lick the sides of buildings, until the hot jagged jaws of fire bite into crystal squares, making them shatter.

Our protagonist feels less invisible and must take refuge. Where? Shop doorways? No, for they are sheltering the dead. Alleyways? No, more bodies lie in the way. The Synagogues are all burning. Even the sacred resting places have not been spared.

The smell of death catches in his throat, but he does not choke, for his breath has already been taken away. He is out of breath, out of words, out of time, out of step, and he will fall in the streets, on the night of broken glass.

'Here was I, in the middle of an
earth-shattering upheaval.'

Chapter 7

No More Windows

After Kristallnacht, my old friends, those thoroughfares became strangers to me. If I were standing in those stricken streets right now, I would tell you that there are no windows that once opened onto the towns and cities that witnessed the chaos and carnage. No windows to let in light and air. No windows to let out the sounds of human habitation. They have been destroyed and the music that once emitted from their gaping mouths has been silenced. And people say, if you look into a piece of broken glass, you will see, not your reflection, but the fierce flames of hatred. But, if you oh, so carefully hold a shard to your ear, like a broken shell, you will hear the faint sound of a violin. Or is it a human voice? It is difficult to say which. They both want to say the same thing; to reassure us, that in the end all will be well.

I suppose there was no escaping; how can I put it? It was a kind of Jewish reality. A Jew had to have broad shoulders; shoulders that carried a burden of blame. It dates back for more than two millennia. And in modern history to quite recent times. This is the blame apportioned to the Jewish people of Germany, for Germany's demoralising defeat on the battlefields of the First World War. The assimilation of Jews into German society was blamed for a perceived decline in German culture. Jewish influences were said to be leading to the country's downfall. That Jewish people were succeeding in professional life, to many it seems, became unacceptable.

I should have paid more heed to my brother. He was right to remind me that decisions over which musicians would keep their jobs were in the hands of the newly formed Reich Chamber of Music. Germany wanted to restore what it considered to be its musical supremacy. This meant that only good German music from the likes of Bach, Beethoven and Brahms could be performed. Jazz, on the other hand, was seen as degenerate music, and was strictly out of bounds.

Here was I, in the middle of an earth-shattering upheaval. It had been gaining momentum since 1933 when Germany's new Chancellor was appointed. I ignored all the landmark events which eventually led to an equally, earth-shattering event in my own life. I shut out the news of Jewish business boycotts, the burning of Jewish literature, the removal of German citizenship. Surely marking a passport with a J, for Jew and compulsory middle names, was just bureaucracy gone mad, and such madness would pass. War was written in mountainous letters right in front of me. So large were these letters, that I could not see them. But it was war. War with my community, my fellow musicians, my friends, and my family. A World at war.

How could things ever be the same for Ari Israel Vander? Things were never the same and I told myself that I would never play the violin again.

'Without music, I was in a kind of wilderness.'

Chapter 8

Out of Love

How could I possibly play the violin if there was no love left in me and if I found it impossible to forgive? And so, there followed a time of estrangement from the instrument. If it had been a living, breathing family member, I would have disowned them; if it had been a family friend or neighbour, and I should see them across the street, I would have crossed over to the other side.

It is at this moment in these recollections that I need to explain to you that between the years 1933 and 1941, there was a period when Jews were granted permission, if you like, to engage in music and theatre. The authorities were persuaded to allow the formation of the Jewish Culture League. It began in Berlin, and rapidly gained a following, which inspired the formation of other similar organisations throughout Germany. It was a means of enabling Jewish artists to earn an income and respite from life's hardships. It was a distraction, a mental means of escape.

I needed an escape too. Without music, I was in a kind of wilderness. Whatever work I could get was always going to be menial rather than meaningful. I needed to express myself, to be a creative being again. Subservience in an armaments factory would hardly allow that. And yet, scholars would no doubt argue, that the formation of the Jewish Culture League was a propaganda tool, which could demonstrate to the outside world that the German authorities were not mistreating the Jews, but providing them with a cultural outlet. Did it enrich Jewish lives, or was it yet another way to keep the Jewish community separate from the rest of German society? Or were Jewish musicians unwittingly collaborating with an enemy?

My dear reader friend, I have no grounds on which to criticise or make a judgement on what the scholars think. I held out for as long as my resolve not to play could last. Alas, it was not long enough for me to claim any kind of personal victory or credit. Had I continued for much longer, I would have been begging on the streets for handouts, and the streets were too hostile for the likes of me and my kind. And so, I went back on my word and joined the Berlin Orchestra. As more and more orchestral musicians managed to scrape the means together to leave Germany for Palestine, there was an ever-increasing number of seats to be filled in the string sections. It was the orchestra of the League in Berlin, which survived the longest. I lived in the fragile protection of the orchestra for a while, but by 1941, Jews could be easily identified in public wearing their compulsory yellow badges. This was to mark them as a religious or ethnic outsider. Germany was, by now, fully immersed in its war effort, and no longer made the pretence of supporting Jewish society. The Jewish Culture League was finally disbanded in August of 1941. By 1943, I was in Auschwitz concentration camp and, once again, I vented my anger on the instrument I once loved.

Again, I call upon you, dear reader, to imagine. Imagine if you can, the sound of footsteps along a gravel path. The crisp disturbance of gravel beneath the soles of boots now changes to the dull clunk of those same boots mounting wooden steps; two sets of boots and two sets of steps to be precise. A wooden door now flies open, and the occupants of the barracks that belong to the door scramble to their feet and form a line, shoulder to shoulder. One of the German SS guards addresses the men.

'Good. That is what I like to see. Respect when an officer enters. And such a beautiful straight line. You learn quickly. Which is also good. I hate to be disappointed. Now to business. Does anybody here play the violin?'

There is no response from any of the men other than their obvious nervousness, given away by their moist brows.

The guard forces a smile and continues, 'Come now, don't be shy. This is no time for false modesty. I will ask again. Does anyone here play the violin? If you do, then please take one step forward and identify yourself.'

Immediately there is a simultaneous shuffle of feet as the entire line of men take an almost comedic step backwards. Well, almost everyone. A single unsuspecting soul finds himself in a position as if he had taken a step forward. The guard is not amused.

'Since when does stepping backwards constitute a single person stepping forwards? I too can play games. Do not tempt me to indulge myself.' He now focuses on the unwitting volunteer. 'Do you play the violin?'

Before the poor man can answer, there erupts a chorus from the remaining men. 'YES!'

The guard's irritation was growing. 'He can speak for himself. Well?'

'I play the violin,' came the unwitting volunteer's barely audible reply. The rest of the line were quick to respond.

'HE IS VERY GOOD!'

'Silence!' cautioned the guard. 'Why did you not speak up when I asked the question? Do you not realise that I could have you punished for such insolence?'

The man was a quick learner, and he realised resistance was not the best or safest way to engage with the guard, so he answered as politely as he could. 'If you please sir, I have no violin.'

The guard feigned a sympathetic gesture as he said, 'Do you hear that? He has no instrument.'

Upon hearing this, the rest of the men felt obligated to respond, and burst into a whole repertoire of mumbles and equally sympathetic gestures. The guard took a deep and measured breath.

'Silence!' He collected himself and once again forced his contorted face into another smile. 'We would not want a lack of instrument to spoil things now, would we? I shall get you an instrument.' With a click of his fingers, he sent his subordinate on an errand which was completed with remarkable speed and efficiency. Back he came with a violin and bow. The guard took the instrument and immediately offered it to the man saying, 'It is a little broken, but it still plays. Now, play.'

Tentatively, and being willed on by a silent but palpable force which was releasing from the men like invisible radio waves, the man began to play. There was a stillness in the barrack room. Neither men nor guards moved a sinew. All listened. Euphoria entered through the closed door and embraced every occupant. The guard waited several seconds after the playing had finished before he spoke.

'You play very well,' he said, trying to sound matter-of-fact. 'Because you played so beautifully, I shall forego administering the punishment.' He raised his chin and tilted his head to one side. 'You may even live a little longer.' Then the guard's tone changed. 'The rest of you shall consider yourselves fortunate that you will be required to stand exactly where you are for the next two hours, by which time you will, no doubt, be wishing that you too could play the violin as well as your friend.' He turned to the musician, 'Now, come with me.'

The men in that barrack room were indeed fortunate on that day, when ordered to stand. The last thing they would have wanted was another period of standing, after having to support their aching bodies on weak legs during evening roll call, but at least they were inside their quarters, and they only had to stand for a further two hours.

Let me explain. After a torturous day's labour, evening roll calls were routinely carried out. At the sound of a gong, detainees would rush outside and assemble in rows in the roll call square. Such was their exhausted state that this rush was choreographed to look as though the gong's calling was eagerly and dutifully accepted. And there was good reason for this. These roll calls could be prolonged if the head count didn't total up to the guard's satisfaction. Roll calls could be spontaneously repeated in the middle of the night. Detainees would be forced to stand to attention for hours, even in inclement weather. Anyone who moved was likely to be sent to the gas chambers, as were those who showed signs of sickness or weakness or depending on the mood of the guard, hence the wisdom in showing eagerness to respond to the gong. A fellow detainee told me that, should this ever happen to me, I must stand as upright as I could, and do everything in my power to appear in health. I should wish myself invisible to the searching eyes of the SS guard and pay no heed to the cold blanket of snow, or the biting wind, or the lashing rain that would conspire to make me yield to the guard's hunger for violence.

Yes, on that day in the barracks, good fortune shone upon those men as they watched the guards escorting the newly discovered musician out to his assignment. As the door clattered shut, they all gave a thankful sigh of relief, but not that you would particularly notice for, remember, they all had to remain standing for two hours and this would be done under the watchful eye of the

Kapo. A Kapo was a detainee who had been given the responsibility to oversee work details in their barracks. They frequently resorted to violence against their fellow detainees and sometimes to greater extremes than some of the guards. Of course, if they had not demonstrated violence, they would have been murdered anyway.

"How do you play your instrument,
not let your feelings show?
The anger I would feel for them would
break me soon I know
I scream inside at everything,
I'm at that moment when
I just don't want to lose it all and hate
things just like them."

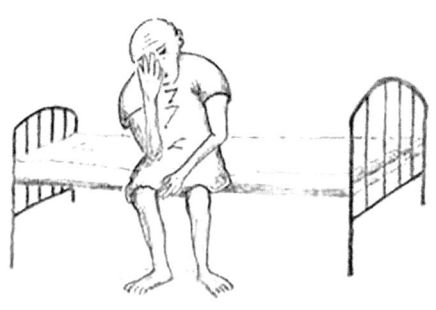

'Sickness however, seemed impossible to evade.'

Chapter 9

Out of Hope

The guard never even asked for the young volunteer's name, despite hearing him play so beautifully. Hmm, now my friend, you are perhaps thinking that his name was Ari? Surely? I was there? Yes, I was there, but I was among those who took a big step back. On that day, just like that reluctant volunteer, I also had no violin, and I certainly wasn't going to own up to being an accomplished player. How could I confess, in the presence of my fellow detainees, to having been a member of the Berlin Orchestra. I could not hurt these people in this way. And yes, they were people; victims of hate; viciously torn away from their properties, their possessions, and their families. We had to be a family now; of a kind that could not be broken. Huh! family. Where were my blood family now? My brother, I believed to be holding his life together across the Atlantic, but as for my parents? No! Do not ask me that question.

At the time of my incarceration, my past association with the Berlin Orchestra and the fact that I had gone back on my word never to play again became my secret burden of shame. In that place, the name of which I still find difficulty in saying, it felt like a suitable penalty in the beginning, for me to be without the instrument. I had no violin, and in that place, I also no longer had a name. Nor did that brave musician. Everyone among that group of detainees knew that calling him Noach in front of the guards would be a very unwise thing. In that place, none of us had a name. Jewish names were no longer the keystone of our identity; they were a millstone; a tombstone.

What an unlikely clean-shaven, showered, and striped-suited sight we became. Know us now, only by the numbers etched into our very flesh. Having a Jewish name was all that was needed for a train ride to hell; standing room only. How I remember that train ride.

Those that had died among us on that long and hideous journey, still stood where they took their last breath, so closely had we been forced together in those dark unventilated cattle cars. When the doors finally opened at our destination, the living spilled out into the night air. The rest crumpled like rag dolls. The blinding light, now the enemy of our past darkness, prevented us from seeing the bodies fall, but we heard them. You never forget the sound of a falling body. Nor do you ever forget the sound a rifle-butt makes when it is rammed against a human side like a butcher's cleaver.

As our surroundings began to materialise, as if out of a mist, I saw a man, desperately holding on to a violin case with one hand and his pregnant wife with the other. Finally, he succumbed to the beatings and released them both. His violin was crushed. Then, we were divided by our captors. The man was directed to the left with me. His wife was directed to the right along with the sick and elderly. We never saw any of them again.

In that place, it took very little time for me to learn how important it would be never to show any signs of sickness. And very soon after that day in the barracks with the music loving guard, I realised that playing the violin gave you at least a slim chance of staying alive. Sickness, however, seemed impossible to evade.

I suspect you might be thinking that the infirmary would be exactly the right place if one needed solace, and so, why would a person want to avoid being there, even if under false pretences. Well, you must remember that concentration camp infirmaries offered little in the way of solace, not to mention sanitation or patient care. And yet, detainees were likely to end up in the camp hospital in their first months of incarceration, if not due to sickness, then due to having been subject to brutal treatment. The sad irony is, that the sickest detainees would find the infirmary a short-cut to the gas chambers; a process known as selection.

The infirmary I found myself in, and certainly not under false pretences, was run by members of the Schutzstaffel, otherwise known as the SS. I remember well that bleak unwelcoming environment as I struggled to sit upright on the edge of my allocated sick-bed, waiting for an SS doctor to assess me.

When the doctor arrived, he carried a clipboard with some papers attached to it and a pen. He stood and looked down at me with indifference and enquired, 'Did no one ever tell you never to get sick? I have enough on my list. See!'

He thrust the clipboard towards me, but I took little notice as I replied, 'I thought it might at least get me a few nights' sleep and a clean comfortable bed.'

The doctor made no eye contact, but with continued indifference enquired, 'And now you are here, what do you make of block twenty?'

Beyond feeling intimidated I offered, 'I've learned that if the rats and fleas don't eat me alive, I can at least let the lice feast on what is left of my flesh before I leave.'

The doctor was somewhat taken aback by my retort. 'Leave?' he quizzed. 'There are two possible pathways by which you can exit. Firstly, I can decide what you will die from.' He held up a limp hand, 'Look at my poor wrist, it hurts almost as much as my brain from having to fabricate so many causes of death and sign so many death certificates. Secondly, you might be granted a privilege reserved exclusively for Jews. You could be selected. Either way, you will eventually be able to leave. Of course, in the event of a miracle, you could recover and be sent back to your work detail. Labour is getting increasingly short, and with the demands placed on our economy due to the war effort, it is in our interests, sadly, to keep some of you alive.'

I tried to make light of the doctor's chilling list of exit pathways saying, 'The options sound interesting. Do I get an audition?'

At last, some emotion from the doctor. 'You fool with me, Jew, as if you had contempt for your own life.'

'That would be true,' I replied, 'if I felt that I even remotely had a life.'

'You are delirious.'

'Then I talk nonsense.'

The doctor was now clearly becoming angry. 'I am beginning to think you talk too much!' Suddenly his mood lightened slightly. He continued, 'I am curious to know why you said that word?'

'What word? I am talking nonsense.'

The doctor gave me what I interpreted as a searching look, but in reality, it was a look of vague recognition. 'Audition. You said audition. Despite your lack of respect and your overt stupidity, you are, shall we say, eloquent, but I would question the appropriateness of such a word in a place such as this.' The doctor's eyes suddenly lit up. 'You are a musician!'

I inwardly shuddered at this remark. I was still carrying my burden of shame. I barked back at him, 'I am a detainee. A nobody. How can I be a musician?'

Ignoring my response, the doctor continued, 'Forbidden music!' He paused to see what effect this statement had on me. 'Mmm, your silence gives you away.' His voice softened. 'Now we are getting somewhere. You play jazz.'

I was horrified to hear him say this. I had been bracing myself to deny any connections with the Berlin Orchestra, but when he mentioned jazz, I could sense my exit from the infirmary beginning to gape open. I needed a response. 'It is forbidden,' was all I could think of saying.

The doctor would not let go of his thought train. 'Violin!' he announced. 'You play violin, and you play forbidden music.'

My heart was pounding. 'I neither like jazz, nor do I play the violin.'

Still, he would not let it go. 'Hamburg!' he declared. The doctor then began to quote part of the closing gambit that we always repeated at the end of an evening's performance, 'You will say to your children, I was there that night, when the world knew not who they were, but it knows now.'

Now he had me, I thought, and I was about to spit out further denials when a suddenly changed doctor drew up a nearby chair and sat close to me by the bed. He now spoke in a whisper.

'You have nothing to fear,' he mouthed. 'I was there…in the audience, listening to music forbidden by the government. But not by me.'

I could hardly believe what I was hearing. 'You like jazz?'

The doctor stifled a laugh. 'Fool, of course I don't like jazz. I love jazz. And you play it. I've seen you. You are gifted. That evening was,' he paused as he searched for the right word, 'sublime.'

'We took a risk,' I ventured.

'We all did. Who wants to be arrested?'

I wondered whether the doctor saw the irony in this remark and quipped, 'I can't imagine.'

'You played with such passion, such energy.' As the doctor said these words, he removed one of the sheets of paper from his clipboard and began tearing it up.

'What are you doing?' I asked.

His reply astonished me. 'Destroying your death certificate.' He swiftly rose from his chair, calling out for the Orderly. In the time it took to rapidly scuffle a pair of frightened feet, the Orderly was in the room and standing to attention. The doctor boomed out, 'What is the meaning of this? You allow one of our patients to lie in his own filth? Clean sheets and a decent pillow this instant, and no more of your stinking food. A good meal for our patient. Is this a hospital or a playground for rats?'

The Orderly was stunned into silence until he was ignited into action by the doctor's final, 'DO IT!'

After the Orderly had scattered like a frightened rabbit, the doctor came close to me again and, in a hushed tone, told me that I would play again and that he should see to it personally. However, it was not to be forbidden music, not just yet, but good German music.

I could equate this to mean only one thing, 'How so? The gate orchestra?'

Bizarrely, detainees who passed an audition were assigned to play in the so-called gate orchestra. Their main responsibility was to play marches as work details departed and returned to the camp.

'You should know that Jews do not qualify for that privilege. No!' The doctor now addressed me in a more friendly but didactic tone. 'We have other, how shall I say…eminent guests in our wonderful hotel. I speak, of course, of one of our female residents in the neighbouring annex to this site. It is fortunate that the commandant of the women's camp is a music lover, and that Jews are now being allowed to participate. You, of course, are extremely fortunate that I shall nurse you back to health, just like I did that exceptional violinist who now leads the women's orchestra. I call her the little flower because of her peculiar habit of searching for them at the perimeter fence. I will arrange a meeting. If she asks you if you can teach, you shall say yes. There is no other way for me to get you into the women's camp.'

I was astonished. My voice dried up, and I grappled for something to say, eventually managing, 'And this woman's name?'

The doctor raised his eyebrows. 'Come now, you know better than to ask me that. She is a Jew.'

*'There was a kind of causeway dividing the
men's camp from the women's camp...'*

Chapter 10

The Fences that Divide

At this point in my narrative, my reader friend, I have to ask a question. It is this. When death is breathing down your neck, do you turn to face it, or do you run? If you are too sick to run, do you crumple and cower, cover your head, and beg for mercy?

At that moment in time when my personal possessions were in the hands of my captors, and my humanity had been diluted down almost equal to the lowly beast of the field, I had little regard for my own life. Any quantity of adrenaline my body may have possessed must have reached its expiry date. The doctor could have done with me whatever he chose to do, and I would have offered no resistance. Why should I care? My liberty had been taken, and my human worth was being peeled away like a skinned carcass. I began to hypothesise, that I must have plotted some monstrous crime to deserve such treatment. I was losing sight of Ari Vander who was, by now, less than a man and who could not even answer to the name, Ari Israel Vander.

Could either of these persons ever be persuaded to play again?

But now, enough of this. Forgive me, this excursion of the emotions. Some feelings run deep, but let me get back to my story.

The doctor was true to his word, although I could not help but think that he must have had some sinister ulterior motive for his outward act of compassion. It took a good while for me to recover my strength, and I sensed the doctor getting impatient with me. Eventually my sickness retreated, and I was able to serve, as I saw it, as his musical marionette in order to provide him with a bit of sport.

There was a kind of causeway dividing the men's camp from the women's camp, with a high impregnable stretch of wire fencing, each side. The SS doctor had enabled a clandestine meeting to take place there between myself and the leader of the female camp orchestra. The doctor was obviously taking a considerable risk in this action. I was escorted to the allocated spot by one of the doctor's subordinates, who waited a little distance away. I had my back to the fence hardly daring to expect the meeting to happen, for my escort was holding a rifle. No doubt, the female escort would be doing the same. The setting, with the two dividing elevations, and flanked by a man on one side, and a woman on the other, was strangely reminiscent of a Jewish wedding where a circle of singing, dancing men would join the groom, and a circle of singing, dancing women would join the bride, and each circle separated by some form of divider.

I had no idea that the person I was meeting was already there, and waiting for me to arrive back into the here and now. Her voice momentarily startled me.

'You have certainly taken your time getting here,' she called. 'I have waited many days for this meeting!'

My eyes were still fixed on my escort's rifle, but I managed a reply. 'Forgive me if my minor incapacity has been an inconvenience for you. I have been told to say yes, if you ask me whether I teach the violin.'

'And do you?' she questioned.

There was only one reply I dared respond with, 'I have been told to say yes.'

'The doctor was right,' she called out, 'you are stubborn!'

I knew how to respond to this remark, 'And you are the little flower.'

I detected almost laughter in her voice as she said, 'I suspected the doctor had a name for me. And what shall I call you?' Trying to get a glimpse of who she was talking to, she added, 'Let me see you! Turn around.'

I was reluctant to oblige but replied, 'If we look at each other, then we shall have to get engaged.'

She now gave a more unrestrained laugh saying, 'Come! Turn around. Let me see you.'

My armed escort suddenly looked less interested in me, and had relaxed his posture a little, so I felt more confident about turning my back on him. Once again, I steeled myself, as I have a habit of doing in times of adversity, and slowly turned around to look beyond the vertical divide. We now faced each other, several metres apart, and with a tangle of hostile wire to obscure our view.

Once in my early life, I experienced what I then described as an aura; something that is generated from one person to another, but which belongs not to the spoken word, nor to the human touch. And yet, it is a form of touch, and a profound form of communication. Instantly, I knew who I was looking at. My next words were an expression of supreme elation. The kind that can bring a person back from death to life.

'Mechayeh!' I cried. 'This cannot be!' I struggled to compose myself. 'Now I am alive,' I exclaimed, with unbridled joy in my voice. 'Rose! It is you. And just as beautiful!'

Rose, the mysterious girl from my boyhood, was in better control of herself than I was, and responded in more moderate tones. 'Hah! The concrete and wire distort your vision, Ari. But yes,' Now there was a warmth to her voice, 'it is good, so…very good -' Rose paused for a moment, for she was trying to resist caving in to her emotions. 'Hah! Good to be able to see you at a distance like it always has been. And this time, looking back at me instead of running away.'

I wanted to tear down those fences, and I cared not whether my escort heard my response. 'If only I could run away, Rose. And take you with me.'

Rose gave a broad smile, saying, 'Careful, Ari, we're only just engaged.'

'Rose! I can hardly believe it.'

Rose's tone became once again more moderate. She looked back, first towards her escort and then across to mine. Both were similarly disinterested in their respective charges, which meant that Rose was safe to continue. 'Believe this, Ari,' she said, 'you are an accomplished teacher and you have agreed to be given access to the women's orchestra on specified days for an indefinite period. Do you understand?'

I obligingly began to repeat what she had said, 'I am an accomplished teacher and I – But for what purpose Rose? The guards will not let me in on a pretence, just so that I can see you. And I don't play anymore. I cannot play anymore.'

I think if Rose could have physically shaken me, she would have done so, 'Ari! Listen!'

My inward anger and disdain began to surface once more. I had misunderstood her, and through gritted teeth I pushed out the words, 'Who listens anymore! We all know what the screams, groans and cries mean.'

Rose ignored the intent behind my comments and continued, 'In the woods. Beyond the perimeter fence. In the woods, Ari. Listen.' For a few moments, Rose made no sound, and then she pursed her lips, and channelled her breath into a series of musical notes that I could not fail to recognise, 'Cuckoo, cuckoo, cuckoo.'

It was a poor imitation, but I knew what it meant. In an instant, I was transported back to my boyhood quest to seek inspiration for my violin playing from the voices of nature. I recalled vividly that time when I played unwittingly outside the window of the house where Rose was staying, and how, upon bending down to collect a coin someone had thrown, I received more than I had bargained for. My anger and disdain melted at this fond memory. 'Hah! Now I should be grateful for a simple kick up the backside.'

'That's better, Ari.' Rose was barely audible now for she clearly did not want our escorts to hear. 'Now, listen. Here is the plan. With your help, I intend to form an orchestra, here in the women's camp. An orchestra of the highest standard. They will be rehearsed with such determination that excellence can be the only outcome. They will become the finest ensemble that the German Officers have ever heard. We will subdue our subduers, and they will fall over themselves to hear their sweet German music.'

This was still a difficult challenge for me. It meant that I had to pick up the violin once more, and we were not on good terms. I turned to make sure that my escort had his attention elsewhere. He did. He was preoccupied in checking the working condition of the rifle he held, so I gave my reply.

'Not German music?'

'Yes, Ari. German music.' She was now becoming quite animated in her excitement. Clearly, this plan of Rose's meant a great deal to her. 'We are going to make them tearful to their own tunes.'

'But why would you do this?' I asked.

'Because, Ari, this will be our passport to better provisions, better clothing, better rations, to some kind of life. You know how it works here. The doctor has both our lives in his hands; and in my hands, I have the lives of every Jewish woman who joins our orchestra. If they can't play, I shall do everything in my power to make them play. Let music work for you too, Ari. And help me. Help me make something positive out of this destruction.'

This precious time with Rose came to an abrupt end. Before I could give answer, I felt a firm hand on my shoulder. The hand wheeled me around and I was unceremoniously marched back to my barracks. I tried on several occasions to twist myself around to get one final look at Rose, but my escort responded each time with a violent push between my shoulder blades, which he executed using the butt of his rifle. I supposed he must have found some pleasure in at last being able to relieve his imposed boredom. I do not think the escort was any wiser to the conversation I had with Rose, but I certainly had much to think about.

"I'm looking for the good things,
though I know about the bad
I'm looking for the miracles,
some beauty that we had
Looking for the wonderful,
that only we can see
Looking for the beautiful
that's found in you and me."

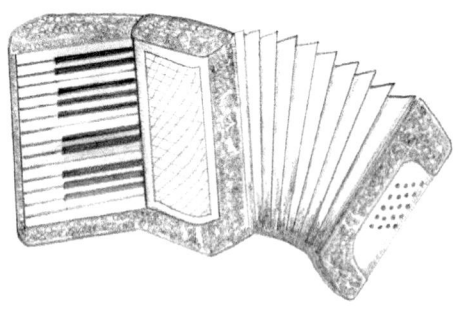

*'Eventually, the thick silence that followed
was broken by the accordion player…'*

Chapter 11

The Gift of a Merry Tune

I was in a state of incredulity after that totally unexpected meeting with Rose. She consumed my thoughts for a good while and most definitely lifted my spirits. So consumed was I, that I never spared a thought as to whether Rose reciprocated my feelings. However, there was little doubt that she was much more in tune with the reality of her circumstances than I was. Whereas I was still in a kind of cerebral limbo; she was in motion, or at least her plans were. She had an inner beauty that her shabby attire and austere surroundings could not suppress, and as I eventually came to realise, much wisdom. Why not let music work for us, especially if it gained us some respite from the hardships and cruelty that had become our normality.

I considered myself fortunate to be given an opportunity to put Rose's theory to the test when one of the SS guards instructed me to work with a family of Romani detainees, in preparation for a concert. Surely it couldn't be that difficult. The Gypsy Family Camp was a neighbouring subcamp. Remarkably, it had its own ensemble of Romani musicians. I had suspected that the SS doctor was not the only German officer with a secret liking for the forbidden music. My suspicions were confirmed when I learned about the Romani ensemble and their forthcoming performance.

Romani people have been scorned and persecuted across Europe for centuries. My younger brother Levi had grown to be quite an authority on Romani music, and I learned much about their musical history from him before he sailed for America. Naturally, as the older brother, I did not want to be, shall we say, upstaged by his advantage over me when it came to Romani particularities. Subsequently, when any of our musical engagements took us within the vicinity of a public library, I would be in there reading up on the Romani way of life. Traditionally, many of them worked as craftsmen, such as blacksmiths, tinsmiths, horse-dealers, and toolmakers. Many earned a living as performers, such as musicians, dancers and even circus animal trainers. Nomadic Roma, were less numerous now, but even the so-called sedentary Romani people would embark on seasonal migrations, depending upon their occupations.

The spirited Romani family that I was given permission to visit, under armed guard, were naturally reluctant to play. It was up to me to lift them out of their reluctance, and to save them from almost certain punishment if they failed to comply. By now, although I had not yet picked up an instrument, I had been copying out music for the women's orchestra. This partial reconciliation between me and the violin, was at least enough for me to muster enough energy to try and revitalise this family of players. When I turned up at their rehearsal barracks, I was pleasantly surprised to have an ally among them.

I had barely walked through the door, when who should come rushing up to me with a greeting, but Noach, clutching his somewhat battered violin and bow. As he embraced me, I managed to glimpse over his slight frame, to see a huddle of round shouldered and limp looking, less than lively musicians, who appeared more than reluctant to pick up and tune their instruments. Noach swept me to one side and offered a word in my ear.

'Looks can be deceiving, Ari. If anyone can do this, I know you can, and I am sure you will be delighted to know that I shall be joining them on short-term loan. They are missing a string player. Look, here is my trusty violin.' Noach continued in more hushed tones, 'Their last violin player made the mistake of asking to be taken to the infirmary.'

Noach now span around and addressed the troupe in a loud voice so that they could all hear. 'Ladies and gentlemen meet the man who is here to work his magic and bring our playing to another level. And then you really will be ready to give a concert of a lifetime.' Before continuing, Noach gave a quick glance in all the directions of the compass. I knew he was about to use my name and was checking for the listening ears of any guards. 'I give you my good friend, Ari.'

A young female was the first to break the embarrassing silence that followed. 'Why should we play for the ears of those who mock our screams when they beat us? Why should we play for the pleasure of those who will murder us?'

I half expected at least some resistance and asked, 'What is your name?'

The woman elevated herself from the chair she was occupying and folded her arms defiantly. 'Nadya!'

I nodded, and took a few seconds to rehearse in my head, what I would say next. 'I met a Nadya once.'

The second female in the room wasted no time in responding. 'Then consider yourself fortunate. Eh! Nadya?'

This retort triggered a simultaneous burst of laughter from the musicians, including Noach.

I shook my head, but more as a sign of appreciation for the joke, rather than in offence from it. After I had collected my dignity, I simply asked, 'Do you know what your name means?' I followed up with the answer, 'It means hope.'

The second female whose name I never learned, came back at me again with, 'Huh! Now we have a poet in the camp.' More laughter rang out, but she had not finished. 'What can you possibly know about our music? Mmm?'

Truly, I was not in the least bit offended, but I was not going to buckle under the strain of this cold encounter. I confidently delivered my answer like the professor of music that one sometimes secretly dreams to be.

'The music of the Romani people can be traced back to northern India, and more recently to Europe. It has a multitude of influences which include Byzantine, Greek, Arabic, Persian and Turkish, to name but a few. Because Romani people have travelled, the parameters of their particular style of music, are difficult to define. There are many differences in melodic, harmonic, rhythmic and formal structures, which vary from region to region. Lyrics are often sung in one or more of the regional dialects of the Romani language, and their musical performances are frequently accompanied by dance.'

Eventually, the thick silence that followed was broken by the accordion player, as he let a hand drop away from one of the straps on the side of his instrument, allowing the bellows to release an embarrassing rasp.

'And furthermore,' I continued, 'I happen to know that Romani people will play much better with decent food in their bellies, and better clothes on their backs.'

Noach could not resist coming in with support, 'And Jews!' he declared.

There was no need for head shaking at this comment. My nod was one of approval. 'And Jews,' I agreed. I had now found my feet. 'Our captors may profit from our pain, but we can profit from their pleasure. Please them, and I guarantee that you will receive better treatment.'

Nadya leaped to her feet. 'Then what are we waiting for! Come family. Let us show the teacher just what we are made of!'

The shackles of lethargy had been broken, and as if a theatre technician had suddenly thrown a switch or pulled a lever at a given cue, the room was alive with movement, melody, and laughter. My head was filled with sounds that took me right back to the woods. The difference was that the laughter was not due to my impersonation of a cuckoo. It was the laughter that only music has the power to evoke. It was cathartic, and every one of us in that room could smell the pine trees of the forest, feel the grass beneath our feet, and if we had been able to keep our hair, we would have felt the summer breeze flowing through it. When the rhapsody finally came to an end, the Romani troupe all stood there with heaving chests. There then followed spontaneous clapping, and back slapping, and imaginary hair ruffling, and you would never have believed that we were all prisoners, with such freedom of expression. But the loud jolting of the barrack door as it burst open rapidly brought us back to our senses.

The guard had obviously been listening outside. I desperately hoped he had not heard us addressing each other by name. It seemed not, and as he strode into the room with his percussive boots, his gloved hands gave us all a muted round of applause. 'Excellent!' he smiled, 'Most excellent. I see your Jewish teacher has made a good start. I shall see to it personally that my gypsy orchestra is rewarded for its efforts.' He now turned to me. 'This will do for now, teacher. You seem to have worked a miracle and injected some life into their veins.'

This statement was a cruel joke which, at the time, none of us would have understood. Trials had taken place, to determine an effective way of killing seriously ill prisoners by injecting highly concentrated solutions into their veins. The most effective killing method was found to be by injection, directly into prisoner's hearts. There was a room in block twenty where this took place.

The guard, with an attitude of indifference that we were accustomed to, then said, 'Now teacher, you shall be escorted back to your barracks.' He then characteristically raised his chin, tilted his head to one side, and looked towards Noach. 'Our deputising violin player on the other hand, has one further engagement before he is dismissed. Being as you played so well for me when you entered this camp, I shall reward you also. I have a rather, special event planned this evening, for which your playing services will be required.'

Noach seemed almost pleased at this show of favour and said that he would be willing and grateful for the opportunity.

The guard gave his signature smile as he declared, 'Then let us waste no further time. Your audience awaits.'

Soon, I was back in my barracks, allowing myself to indulge in at least a tiny portion of self-satisfaction and triumph. Noach was duly escorted to his next musical engagement.

"Looking for the hopeful flower,
listening for that sound
Searching for the melody
that no-one else has found
For hidden in this mystery
is something I must say
From somewhere deep down in my heart,
so this is why I play."

'When you play the violin, you are somebody.'

Chapter 12

The Fences that Unite

Those precious moments with the Romani troupe had been exhilarating and had reminded me just how powerful music was at crossing cultural divides and bringing people together. Not only that, but it was a means of escape from deprivation and pain. Like a miracle cure, it could restore body and mind, let alone nourish the soul. It was like a bridge between heaven and earth. It was unchained joy.

Well, that's how I felt as I was marched back to my barracks, and nothing my escort could have said or done would have made me deny it. At the barracks, for the first time, I actually picked up and held the instrument that the SS doctor had somehow procured for me. It was obvious that it had once been the property of a competent musician. I could tell by its condition that it had been cared for. I also suspected that this previous owner, whoever they were, was no longer alive. But I could not let this thought suppress my new resolve. Something in me began to rekindle, and I felt that just perhaps, it was time for me to play again. Playing for my own gratification was out of the question, and had I done so, I would surely have felt an enormous wave of guilt. Such feelings can dwell within a person for a good length of time, if not a lifetime, and opening a violin case would be like opening a wound.

It has been reported that, after the war, some musicians never played again. German-made instruments were destroyed by some players or sold for far less than their monetary worth. It made no difference that the German instruments were probably of equal quality to some Italian or French examples. But I had been uplifted by that Romani family, and although my Luthier's eye told me that the instrument I had been allocated was German-made, I sensed that it was somehow speaking to me. It was asking me not to judge it for having German origins. It was stating its case for being of equal quality to other makes of violin but, through no fault of its own, it was carrying the guilt of the hands that had corrupted it. It had been abused, but this did not change its physical makeup; what it was made from. It was a product of the earth and the result of years of growth, touched by the seasons. In the time it had spent as a living thing, it had weathered storms and had finally been cut down by the hand of man. Against this violation, it bore no grudge, for the hand of man had also come to rescue it. Now, as an instrument so beautifully and lovingly crafted, it had become the only instrument to rival the human voice. It breathed and lived again. It held no grievance for what it has suffered. It forgave.

My newly fuelled flame of enthusiasm was, however, soon gutted, and my next meeting with Rose was even more uncomfortable and awkward than the first had been. Let me put it this way. By the time I had arrived at Auschwitz, living, or should I say existing, had been made a little more tolerable with the luxury of wooden bunks on which to spread a straw-filled mattress and beg for sleep to come. On my bunk, the night before I was due to meet Rose again, I succeeded in getting hardly any sleep, and my conscience bit me more than the fleas did. It had been folly for me to heap so much responsibility onto the broad back of music; folly to imagine it ever forming a bridge between heaven and earth. I was not on any bridge. I was on a tightrope.

Once again, the SS doctor had arranged for Rose and me to meet at the two dividing fences. With some of the restrictions being relaxed a little, visits between acquaintances in other blocks was allowed. My meetings with Rose, however, were still organised by stealth. The reason for this, I can only imagine, was because the doctor derived a peculiar portion of pleasure from it. But meet we did.

It was a similar picture as before. We were both under armed escort, but this time we were more confident about turning our backs to them and facing each other. Rose was the first to speak. She opened proceedings by complimenting me on my improved time keeping. I was pleased to see her, but I was stung by her comments relating to the SS doctor. It would seem that he had informed her as to my progress with the Romani orchestra, telling her that I had apparently made quite an impression. She asked me whether I had changed my mind about helping her with her plans for the women's orchestra; had I finally undergone a change of heart. I made no answer to her enquiries, but, in my head, I was trying to prevent myself from telling her that my heart had been changed about many things.

There was a prolonged silence between us, until Rose gave in to her instincts to probe me further and said, 'No need for modesty, Ari. Do you not see the good you have done? Why do you hesitate so? Join us. Help me to save lives.'

I was staring at the ground all this time, but this plea from Rose incensed me. My head was now up and so was my blood. I hissed out my words like a fiery dragon. 'Save lives you say! Save lives!' I was fighting back tears by this time. She obviously did not know the truth about the Romani troupe, but I was in no mood to hand out any sympathy to her, and I was in no frame of mind to receive any praise. Things needed to be said. 'Do you know what they made Noach do after he was escorted from the Romani barracks?' I demanded. I gave Rose no time to answer. 'He was instructed to play the violin while they hanged a man.'

Now, Rose and I were standing stock still; a separated duo as if in a roll call that could end in disaster for the one who moved first or showed any signs of weakness. Was it courage to keep silent, or greater courage to speak? The one with the greater courage spoke first. It was Rose.

'And you feel bad for him?' she asked, in the kind of neutral tones that one expects to hear from a comforting mother. Despite my abrasiveness, Rose remained in control of her emotions, and was almost business-like during our exchanges.

Comfort was not what I was seeking. Rose's tone made me even more angry, but I had not lost the sense of where I was, and what my escort might do if I began to act with even the slightest sign of violence, so I gave a more measured response. 'I feel bad for me.' I was hurting and I wanted Rose to know it. This was a dangerous hurt. In battle with my own conscience, I was so close to deliberately doing something to provoke the guard into aiming his rifle in my direction after what had happened. It was the sight of Rose, only a short distance away, that kept me from doing so. There was more to this Romani story to tell. To tell it, a person must survive long enough to do so.

Rose clearly did not know this story and shaking her head said, 'I don't understand. Why do you behave so?'

To my shame, I was still attacking her, and now came a most accusatory remark. 'Have you sold your soul Rose? How could Noach do such a thing?'

If my outpourings had hurt Rose's feelings, she did not show it. What she did do was to plead with me to speak plainly, so I did, but not before some self-control had returned. This was no time to fall apart. My behaviour could put both of us in jeopardy and I returned to the realisation that I had to tread carefully, and make sure that neither of our escorts was listening. I explained to Rose just how much our first meeting had inspired me, once I had thought things over, and overcome the shock at meeting her. I told her that she had really made me believe that making music could put a little more food into people's mouths, and better clothes on their backs.

Rose half whispered, half called, 'It is true.'

'It was a lie.' I half called; half shouted. Now we both shot a glance at our respective escorts.

Thankfully, both were indulging in what seemed to be their favourite pastime of inspecting their firearms as if they were new toys.

Our voices were now becoming hoarse from trying to restrain our exchanges, and the emotion still welling up inside me made it even harder for me to speak, but I somehow managed to continue. The words were not ones I ever wanted to utter, but as I have already said, there was a story that needed to be told. When I finally said the next three words, I thought my heart would stop.

'The Romani orchestra.'

A confused smile now forced itself onto Rose's face. 'You worked with them. The Doctor told me. He said you made an impression. Did they put on their concert?'

'Oh yes,' I replied, 'after which they were duly rewarded.'

Rose sustained her smile. 'There you are,' she encouraged, 'you set them on their way for better food and at least a change of clothing. You were the one who helped them, Ari.'

It was impossible for me to find a way to sweeten my reply. 'I did help, Rose,' I said, 'I helped send them to their deaths.' Rose was not smiling now, and I could see she was deeply shocked at this statement. 'It's true Rose,' I continued, 'all of them, that same evening. They were sent to the gas chambers.'

How Rose held herself together I shall never know. Eventually she asked, 'And what of Noach?'

I replied, 'He sits in a corner of the barracks clutching a blanket, rocking back and forth. But he is not praying, he's weeping.'

Our escorts had unwittingly granted us the comfort of an unhindered meeting, and it was likely that very soon they would realise this and get bored with inspecting their rifles. Both Rose and I knew that we could not expect much more time at the fence. Rose stepped up the pace. Emotion had no place as her running partner.

She came as close to her side of the fence as she dared, and virtually ordered me to go to Noach, pick him up, and tell him that he should celebrate what he had done.

I was horrified to hear her say such a thing. I said as much, and told her that she was now mocking me.

Rose was adamant. 'Call it what you will, Ari,' she returned, 'but I tell you this, when Noach played at the man's execution, he played like never before.'

I huffed at this, and was still convinced that she was mocking me. It was my turn to get as close to the fence as I dared. 'You weren't there! How could you know?'

It was the mother-like Rose who replied to my retort. 'I didn't need to be there to know.' She then spoke a Yiddish phrase which refers to a kind of spark inside a Jew which is always there, the essence of each individual Jew. She said, 'Pintele Yid, Ari. Pintele Yid.' She continued, and I swear I could almost hear my own mother's voice. 'It took chutzpah to do what he did. Nerve, Ari, a supreme self-confidence. His Jewishness could not be extinguished, and he stood up for that. Do you think it was easy for him? No! Of course it wasn't. But because of who he is, I know this,' her diminutive figure obscured by two fences now looked so strong and determined as she continued, 'Noach saw an opportunity that no human form of incarceration could suppress. He played beautifully and sent that innocent victim of cruelty towards heaven with the nearest thing to the sound of a kind and comforting human voice in his ears. The violin.'

Now it was my turn, but I was less tender. 'Violin you say. All I can hear is the voice of death screaming in my ears. I hate the violin, I should be dead, with the gypsies.'

Rose remained calm and authoritative. 'Perhaps you should, Ari.' She then softened again and became almost like a little girl, adding, 'after all, a violin should be played with love or not at all.'

I heard these words, but they did not entirely register, for I was still angry and indignant, 'Love?' I said, coldly. This was a word and a concept that was in considerably short supply in these environs.

Rose had more to say. 'When you play the violin, you are somebody.'

Even in my bitter and confused state, there was no mistaking the identity of the person who had said these words to me in what seemed a very distant past. I doubt whether the words had originated from his lips, but I had not forgotten them. I managed to regain control of my dropped jaw to exclaim, 'Mr Spielman!'

Rose was now smiling once more, and for the briefest of moments it was as if the barbed wire and concrete had disappeared, and there was nothing to separate us. Her lips formed more words that I had heard as a child. 'Learn to play the violin, and it will teach you to forgive.'

We were both smiling, as children do when given a pleasant surprise. This woman continued to amaze me. 'You did go to the same teacher,' I gasped. Rose nodded, but I had not finished. 'These are wise words Rose, but I am not he. I have become a nobody. I am filled with hate for the instrument. How can we play for them,' I made a surreptitious gesture towards my escort, 'our captors? How is this possible? They that applaud us with the same hands that beat us. They dance to our tunes and tap their feet and with those same feet, kick us into the dirt.'

Rose answered me with more urgency in her voice. We were in serious danger now of over-stretching our allocated meeting time. 'Remember the wine, Ari?' she urged.

I was getting nervous and just repeated what she said, 'The wine?'

She went on, 'At the wedding all those years ago? The wine made from the grape gladdens the heart, but in order to produce this heart gladdening drink, a grape must first be crushed. Life will have its crushing moments, but when people come together, these crushing moments can be overcome.'

My mind suddenly began to play tricks on me. I chanced a glance over my shoulder to check what my escort was doing, and thought I saw the rabbi who had presided over the wedding. I was there again, a young boy in wide-eyed wonder. It was an image that all too soon faded. Wonder changed places with wretchedness. I turned back to Rose, who must have stooped as I did so to pick up a tiny flower she had found.

'Look at this fragile flower, Ari.'

Disappointed at what I thought to be a completely inappropriate remark, considering we were by now, most definitely putting ourselves in jeopardy, I hastily accused her of picking flowers for her hair when she should have been picking them for the graves.

She was undeterred. 'Look at it, Ari. Look!' She held it up, but I could barely see what seemed like an insignificant weed to me. 'Fragile, yet beautiful.' I was ready to walk away, but she would not stop. 'In gentle hands it is not crushed. In hands that wear the golden band it becomes a wedding bouquet. In loving hands Ari, a violin becomes a marriage between the player and the instrument itself. Isn't that worth living for?'

Rose then astonished me even further by trying to pass the flower to me through the fence. 'Take it,' she said. 'Through the wire.' She paused, before admitting, 'I know, impossible.'

I was beginning to feel pity for Rose, and thought that it was not only I who had succumbed to strange fancies of the mind, but she persisted. 'Yes, impossible. Then imagine it, Ari. Imagine it. Close your eyes and take it from me.'

At last, the veil lifted. This gesture had an immediate effect on me. My mood completely changed, and I suddenly felt an overwhelming connection with Rose. Finally, I was beginning to understand what she was really saying, but which she did not want the escorts to be party to. I obediently did as she asked. I closed my eyes and imagined myself reaching out and taking the flower from her. In my new state of understanding I opened my eyes and could see that the flower was very real, and very beautiful. I told her so.

'I have it. It is beautiful.' I now bid her to close her eyes and to imagine me finding a special place to plant the delicate flower. A safe place where it could live and grow.

She obliged, and then opened her eyes and looked over at the ground against the fence where I stood. 'I see it, Ari,' she said.

We both stood there, and again the fences were gone and we were strong again. I cared little whether any of the guards heard me as I called out to her, 'Each time I pass this way, I will look for it and think of you.' I did, however, lower my voice before I continued, but I spoke with a new-found confidence, 'Now, I must make ready to go, before my escort gets too suspicious.'

Before I finally turned away, she called across to me in a clearly articulated form of whisper, 'Ari, the letters SS now stand for something new,' she paused for effect, 'sowing seeds.'

There was only one response that I could make. 'And that is exactly what I intend to do.'

*'Eager hands and arms had already escorted me
to the chair…'*

Chapter 13

Bridging the Divide

I finally got to cross those dividing fences shortly after that notably memorable meeting with Rose, when the seed of greater prospects began to germinate. The optimistic Ari of old was beginning to return. I say this, but you would not recognise me by my appearance, and I was constantly reminded that, in this place, I had no name.

I worked with Rose at every given opportunity. The SS doctor was generous in this regard, and yet I still could not help but think that Rose and I were pawns in a potentially deadly game. I dare not permit the thought that he could have had a trace of humanity dwelling within him. Rose and I would not have to deviate very far from the business of producing music, to be eyed with suspicion. After the Night of Broken Glass, in the winter of 1938, when buildings burned and human lives were extinguished, suspicion was all that was needed for a Jew to be arrested. In this place, there was only one possible outcome for a detainee demonstrating signs of suspicion.

During my time enjoying the company of Rose and working with her orchestra, pangs of guilt sometimes entered my nightmares. These dreams featured a spitting steam locomotive carrying human freight, compressed into dark spaces like rotting fruit. The engine had a name on the side; Iron-heart. I was haunted by its image. In the dream I see a man desperately trying to hold on to his distraught pregnant wife with one hand and his violin with the other. When I first saw that man, among the confused and frightened faces as we were herded like dangerous wild beasts from our wheeled cages, it was a harsh and despicable reality. It was a reality that meant certain death if you were directed to the right and a kind of living death if you were directed to the left. Oh, how I wish it had been a nightmare. At least I could have woken up from it and made my escape. The cruel circumstances of that night when we arrived at the camp, rendered him totally incapable of intervening. He had no bargaining power with which to save his wife. Yet here I was, conspiring with Rose, and using our instruments as mediators for leniency. I once accused Rose of selling her soul, but perhaps I was selling mine.

Rose's gritty determination could not be overstated. Because of her playing prowess, she was held in high esteem by the SS guards. She was as strict and thorough as she was talented. It seemed impossible to think that she could fail in her mission. It was all I could do, even as an accomplished player, to keep up with her. As I spent more and more time with the women's orchestra, still under armed guard I might add, the improvement in the women's playing and appearance became more and more evident. They enjoyed special privileges, such as daily showers and regular changes of uniform and, of course, better food rations. They were also spared any arduous work and thus, being able to concentrate their energies into rehearsing, developed into a most excellent ensemble and all due to the inspired leadership of Rose.

In some ways, it could be argued that the women's orchestra became too good. Aside from playing at the camp gates each morning and evening, they were sometimes expected to play at Sunday concerts and at times when high ranking officials visited the camp. I supposed that the Sunday concerts must have been the most rewarding, as these were for the benefit of some of the detainees and, of course, an audience of camp staff members.

Despite being such a taskmistress, I found Rose easy to work with. What I did find difficult was extracting any information from her concerning her background. I was intrigued to know how she happened to be attending that wedding at which I had spent most of my time clinging to my mother's side, asking questions, and at which Rose and I had exchanged a fleeting glance. Apparently, she was visiting relatives who lived in the same village as myself, and with whom she was staying for a while. Had it not been for such serendipity, I would never have, shall we say, bumped into her, or rather, bumped into the door of the house where she was staying when I received that mighty kick up the backside.

I was somewhat surprised when she admitted that, unlike me, she was not staring in awe at the musicians playing at that wedding celebration. She told me that she was simply studying the fingering technique of one of the players. By the time I was sending my music teacher Mr Spielman to sleep with my monotonous cuckoo impersonations, Rose had completely mastered the art of violin playing and already had a special relationship with it.

Exactly how she came to be a detainee in the women's camp, was never really touched upon by Rose. From her point of view, it was enough that I should know that she and her family had tried to exit Germany at some point during the increasing unrest. They achieved this for a short while and managed to get as far as England's capital. By this time, she was a highly regarded player in elite musical circles and wanted to resume her career. She decided to make an eastward journey. This was her undoing. Upon arriving in France, she was arrested and eventually deported to Auschwitz.

At the beginning of her incarceration, Rose had become very ill, but I know nothing of the cause of her illness. As you can by now appreciate, once her playing prowess had been discovered by the SS doctor, it was almost inevitable that she would receive the necessary treatment to make her well again. The other SS officers also held her in high regard, and she was given the position of Kapo of the music block. It goes without saying that Rose did not observe the pattern of behaviour often displayed by other detainees holding this status. Instead, she ploughed her energies into improving living conditions for her fellow detainees. It began by first convincing the women's camp administration to exempt members of the women's orchestra from having to perform outside during inclement weather. She also engineered a way to get any sick musicians who ended up in the infirmary spared from the process of selection. There was little doubt, that Rose's interventions saved lives. It was now my turn. As a young boy, I remember formulating a plan of action in a quest to find the mystery girl I had seen at a wedding. Who could possibly have imagined, that as an adult, I would be formulating a plan of action, in circumstances almost beyond the imagination with that very same person.

There was still an atmosphere of despair and defeat in my barracks. Not all were musicians, and even those that were had not exploited their talent to gain better favour from the guards. Perhaps I should put this in a more respectful, sensitive, and less judgmental way; not all had understood the power that they each possessed. It was a power that could give them a better chance of survival. And, if we were really creative, we could introduce others to music, teach them to play, or even get them to mingle with our ensemble and pretend to play. Who among us would care, so long as it made our chances of survival stronger?

I had been witnessing and administering this power of which I speak for long enough through my privileged position within the women's orchestra, and it was time for me to express my gratitude by intervening on the other side of the wire divide. On the occasion I recall to you, I had just returned to my barracks, after supplying Rose with some scores I had written out to help with extending her orchestra's repertoire. I knew that I could not waste any more time. Time was not on our side. But music would be, or so I decided on my march back from the women's camp. As I walked and sometimes stumbled, partly due to my ill-fitting clogs and partly due to the prods of the impatient guard, my violin case swung in my hand. The swinging handle squeaked out a repetitive tune. This tune had a lyric that sang out the words, 'Don't delay, don't delay, don't delay, don't delay.'

I entered the barracks with my violin case tucked under an arm. There was a rustling of movement, as those who had the energy and the interest began to sit up in their bunks to welcome me back with a sardonic ripple of applause. This had become a kind of ritual, which I graciously accepted. I saw it as a necessary outlet for some of the men's disapproval, or perhaps envy, at my excursions beyond the two dividing fences. I dealt with this in my usual way and ventured a modest if not theatrical bow.

'No need for applause my brothers. There's nothing heroic about delivering copies of music to the women's orchestra.' As I raised my head, it was impossible not to observe that some of the facial expressions were inconsistent with exhaustion. 'I can see that not all of you approve.' I met the eyes of one of my less supportive bunkmates. 'And there was no funny business, Mendel. I was with a chaperone throughout.'

Mendel looked less accusatory at this, and lightened a little, saying, 'Some Chaperone who carries a rifle, eh boys?' A few of the others managed a weak laugh, and I think Mendel at least tried to further lighten the mood among the men. He turned to one of the detainees who was sitting alone and staring blankly at the floor. He addressed the man. 'Hey! Noach, look who's back. You can come out from under your blanket now.'

I had noticed Noach's withdrawn form on the edge of his bunk and wrapped in a blanket as soon as I had stepped into our quarters. He was in obvious distress, and I did not want to draw attention to this. I knew that he too had his own nightmares to deal with, but I hadn't realised just how fragile his state of mind was. I took Mendel to one side to enquire, 'How long has he been like this?'

Mendel gave me a serious look. 'Long enough for us to have to keep an eye on him, Ari. Look at him.' We both turned our heads just enough to see Noach's pendulum-like motions, made all the more sinister looking with his improvised blanket cloak with which he tried to conceal himself. 'In this state, Ari, he could do anything.' Mendel now positioned himself to address the room. He was again trying to lift the atmosphere of gloom that was growing in our quarters. I was impressed with this unexpected support. 'Well now, seeing as we have our teacher back, I suppose that he would be willing to tell us one of his stories. What say you, Mordechai?'

Mordechai was usually in better spirits and eagerly responded. 'Mordechai says, well said. It'll help us sleep.' He then looked teasingly at me. 'What do you say, Ari? Eh! We are all so very tired. Some of us have been doing real work.' This remark produced much laughter, albeit it weary and sluggish sounding. After it had settled, he drew up a chair from beneath our crude plank-like eating table and gestured for me to sit. 'Take us somewhere,' he implored.

Mendel offered back-up and bellowed, 'Take us anywhere as long as it is away from here!'

As the men began to show signs of coming round, some sitting more upright in their bunks, others planting themselves on a chair, I bid them to wait a moment while I put away my violin, telling them, 'Once I have put away one instrument, then I shall prepare the other one.'

'Ah!' sang out Mordechai. 'The violin and the human voice. Which is which?'

I turned to him and sang back, 'Who can tell, Mordechai. Who can tell?'

All this singing was a cue for Yochanan to express his characteristic impatience, 'You can tell, Ari! Get on with telling your story!' I was surprised that Yochanan was still wake. He was usually the first to collapse onto his itchy mattress.

My anecdotes and reminiscences were well known throughout our barracks, and there was no way that my potential listeners would relent having made a request for another. I had to think of something quickly, but nothing came immediately to mind. It had to be something cheerful and uplifting. There wasn't much time. Eager hands and arms had already escorted me to the chair. I spun it around and straddled it, like one would when using an old-fashioned library reading chair, resting my forearms on the backrest. I had to start, even if I didn't quite know where I was going.

I began, 'There was once a young boy,' I paused, trying to think of the next line. It came, 'A Romani boy and his name was…' I suddenly recalled the name of the Romani leader who had grabbed me by the collar when I stumbled upon his encampment in the woods near my village, way back in my tender youth, 'Nicu,' I declared. 'Nicu, which means victor of the people.'

So far, I felt I had made a good start, and I was sure that my understanding of the meanings of names would impress them. At least I could tell that Mendel was impressed, for he said as much.

I continued with my story. 'Nicu loved to hear his mother sing at the spinning wheel – '

An enthusiastic Mordechai jumped in, 'Was she beautiful? And did she prick her finger and fall into a deep sleep?'

My reply was a cautious, 'Very intuitive Mordechai. But no.' I picked up my pace. 'On the other side of the village, where the boy lived, was the house of a wealthy plantation owner. On some days, Nicu would walk there, barefooted, for he was too poor to own any shoes.' I heard some of my listeners give a deep sympathetic sigh at this, so I knew I was drawing them in. 'The point of his journey was to get a glimpse of the owner's daughter.'

Now, Mendel interjected, 'For she was very beautiful and he loved her.'

'He was eight years old,' I pressed, at which laboured laughter filled the space once more. I went on. 'The daughter played the piano.'

I really should have known better, and after the ooh's and ah's of disappointment had faded, I corrected myself. 'She played the violin.'

Order was restored and there were nods of approval in abundance after which, they beckoned me to continue. 'Her teacher accompanied her on the piano. Now, Nicu so loved the music that he wanted to join in. But how could he? He had no instrument –'

Now Mordechai came back in stating, in no uncertain terms, 'And he was trespassing. He should have got a beating!' More laughter erupted.

Mendel came to the rescue, 'But he did have an instrument. His voice.'

'You have it Mendel!' I exclaimed with delight, and then carried on. 'Forgetting himself one time, in rapture with the music, the boy began to sing. Teacher and pupil exchanged glances. They nod to each other, and whisper, "Pianissimo."'

Mordechai was back, and boomed out, 'Which means quiet!'

Even my patience was being tested now. I could not help but demand, 'Which is what you need to be Mordechai, if you want me to finish this story!' He looked at me. I looked at him and we both simultaneously squeezed a smile, and raised our eyebrows, before I continued. 'Through the softness of their playing, the boy's voice filled the air. He must have sung so sweetly – '

Yet another interruption came, this time from Yochanan. 'How do you know this?' he enquired.

I flattered myself with the thought that my story must have been a good one, because Yochanan had managed to keep sleep at bay. 'Because, Yochanan,' I offered, by way of explanation, 'when he had finished, the girl went outside, ran over to him and kissed him on the cheek.'

'And then he got a beating,' appealed Mordechai, to more groans and laughter.

I eventually became encouraged by the interruptions. The quips and comments were gradually sweeping despondency out of the door, which is where I needed it to be, if I was to finally outline to them, my plan of action. I could not disobey the orders that my swinging violin case handle had squeaked out at me. 'Don't delay,' it persisted. At least I was trying.

As quickly as my frail body would allow me, I stood, whipped the chair around to its more conventional position, sat back down and eased myself a little nearer to the front edge. It was purely a theatrical device to try and gain their fuller attention. I think it worked, so I continued, 'This did not go unnoticed by the music teacher.'

Yochanan, who, in the opinion of many in those barracks, was far too alert to allow my safe passage into storyland, was determined to cause eyes to roll in mounting but harmless frustration, and asked, 'The kiss you mean?'

I tried not to smile as I answered, 'The singing Yochanan! The singing!' I was in danger of falling off my seat by now in my eagerness to complete my story. 'Forget the kissing will you! The singing.' I held back for a moment, steadied myself, and continued. 'It was at that moment that the boy's dream became a reality.'

'To marry the girl,' Mordechai cooed.

Yochanan was obviously giving the story his full attention and came back at Mordechai before I could. 'She was eight years old Mordechai. And you have already been told once to be quiet.' There came a barrage of shushes and a flurry of pointing fingers aimed in Mordechai's direction, but I don't think they registered. However, general goodwill still prevailed. I sat quietly for a moment wondering whether to continue, when Mendel gave me the go-ahead.

'The dream, Ari? The dream?'

'To learn the violin,' I announced. 'And he would pay his fees, simply by singing. He was a good student. He was as quick as he was talented. A child prodigy. And he worked hard. Nothing was too difficult for him. The teacher was so pleased with the boy's progress, that he gave him a brand new violin, as his reward.' After this last declaration, I waited for my applause, but before a single hand could find its opposite and join with it like a fleshy cymbal, Mordechai, stole my moment.

'Huh! I would have settled for another kiss.'

Mordechai's theft of my thunder received a collective, if not synchronised, 'SHUT UP,' which I am pleased to report, was followed by an equally collective round of guffaws. Did I say collective? Well, not quite so. Amidst the hubbub, the blanketed Noach, had risen to his feet and called across to me. His voice was harsh and absent of any energy.

'What is the point of your story, Ari? How can you be like this? Telling fairy stories after all that has happened.' He now turned to Mordechai. 'And you, Mordechai, you joke about beatings!'

Mendel assumed his self-appointed referee role again. 'Ah, look. Now your noise has woken Noach.' Mendel had become a good referee, and he was aware that he could not dismiss what Noach had said. It would have been in unforgivably poor taste to joke about beatings. 'And maybe he is right, Ari,' he said turning to me. 'However hard we work, and however beautiful we make our music, our reward will only ever be another beating or a trip to the infirmary. And we all know what that means.'

There was a grim realisation around the room, for we all knew exactly what going to the infirmary meant. But now, the wide awake Yochanan entered the exchanges. 'What Mendel says is true! More food?' He fashioned a mocking gesture, which looked almost clown-like as his thin limbs appeared to rattle within the baggy material that masqueraded as a uniform. 'Huh! Better clothing? Sure! They just make us burn all the better when they throw our bodies into the incinerator.' He now looked over at Noach who was still clutching his blanket. 'Go on, Noach. Have your say.'

Noach cast off his blanket, and made several steps towards where I was sitting. I instinctively stood up and placed the chair between us. His eyes were no longer full of tears. They were full of fire. I had never seen him like this. His voice was acid.

'I will, Yochanan! I will. What has come over you, Ari? How can you talk as if the world is so full of promise?' He rotated his body around, gesturing to all who were within sight and sound of this strange form of entertainment we were providing. 'How can you even think such a thing, as if we have a future!'

Here was my cue. This was no time to betray the directive that my squeaking violin case handle had given me. I charged. 'I'll show you how!' Now it was my turn to rotate, and demand everyone's attention. 'Stand up! All of you! I forbid you to sit. Do you hear me. Stand!'

Heads were now either turning left to right, or peering over other heads, or around corners to make sense of my outburst, but it was Noach who tried to brush off my out-of-character display. 'What kind of meshuggeneh childishness is this?'

The echoed words of my brother at Cuxhaven port, produced a wry smile upon my face. 'Hah!

You are not the first person to call me crazy Noach.' I faced him, square on. 'Pick up that chair.' Noach did not respond, so I repeated my command. 'Pick up that chair. Now!'

An incensed Noach huffed at me and gritted his unsightly teeth. 'I do the guard's bidding for fear of my life. But not for the likes of you!'

Before Noach had even finished these words he violently kicked the chair to one side and made a grab at my clothing, whereupon he immediately released one hand, and drew it back into a fist, aimed level with my face. I had my defence at the ready and flung out a volley of well-aimed words. 'Go on, Noach. Go on! Fight me, hit me, come on, Noach! Let's fight! We cannot hurt each other. We are too weak…like children.' He relaxed both his hold and his fist, and I pushed him towards the chair. 'Now, pick up that chair.' He was about to protest but I cut him off. 'And before you dare to compare me with one of the guards, remember that I used your name…Noach.' He knew what I was coming to, but I continued, 'which means? Which means?'

Noach had to answer, but he had been subdued. 'You know what it means, Ari. It means released.'

Mendel had not deserted his post as mediator, but he struggled to find something to say. 'You chide us like children, Ari.'

I placed a hand on his shoulder and did the

same to Noach. 'Yes, Mendel,' I said, 'I do.' Now I turned to the muted onlookers. 'Not for being disobedient, but for giving up.' Some tried to respond to this, but I motioned them to stop. I righted the chair, stood next to it and began to deliver a new story. I asked them, 'Were you never chided by your parents for something they forbade you to do? No? Did you never find it impossible to crush that overwhelming desire to reach into that out-of-reach cupboard for that which was forbidden to you?' I mimicked a worried mother's words, 'Get down from that chair, Ari. You'll fall one day and hurt yourself, and that will be the end of you. And then what will you say?'

Mordechai could not resist but join in the roleplay. 'I'll say nothing Mam-e for I shall be dead.' There was a tentative ripple of relieved laughter.

This was no time to make light remarks. I continued. 'Eventually, of course, you give up climbing on chairs. Why? Because my brothers, you grow tall enough to reach for what you want.' I held out my hands, as a conductor does when about to invite his orchestra to stand and take a bow. 'Look at us. On the outside like weak and terrified children. Perhaps we are. But my brothers, broken on the outside we may be, but not inside,' I beat my breast, 'not in here.' As I looked at their pathetic pale and weathered faces, my throat tightened and my heart went out to them, but I had to complete my story. 'My dear brothers, I want to be that child again.' I flung out an accusatory hand, indicating the world outside our barracks. 'What parents are these; our captors, that starve us and humiliate us? Defy them. Stand on that chair. Reach up for what seems impossible to grasp. And even if they kick away that chair, pick yourself up and reach again. And if you can't pick yourself up, claw the ground and crawl if you have to. Summon every last bit of strength you have left in your body and heave yourself back up. Never! Do you hear me? Never let them deny you your right, given to you by your creator, to be human – inside,' again I thumped my breast which tried to contain my heavily beating heart, 'right here, a place that they will never reach.'

'Over the years I have perhaps expended too much energy in trying to justify the SS doctor's behaviour…'

Chapter 14

Minions or Maestros

Please, dear reader, do not put me down as any sort of hero at what I did that evening in the barracks. There have been many who have done much more than I, and who were already in their own campaign for clemency. I suppose you could say that music flowed where it could and squeezed itself between the thin space which kept death just out of reach.

Other ensembles were formed at the behest of the camp administrators. Impromptu ensembles often had to perform at private parties. Dear reader, you must find it strange to contemplate the atmosphere of a party in such surroundings. The notion is completely incongruous with life in a concentration camp. But our music must have possessed powers that we were unaware of. Even covert jazz concerts took place. Some officers would risk visiting certain barracks where they knew musicians who could play jazz were being held. This secret love that some of the guards had for the forbidden jazz proved to be another lifeline for musicians, including me. Yes, I was going to play jazz again. I knew, however, that musicians were not indispensable, and they could be as prominent as they could be scarce. I called this the tunesmith's turnover. This was my weak and bleak attempt at trying to make light of the situation.

There were still occasions when we were subjected to reassignment and put to work, albeit slightly less exhausting work than those who were marched out of the gates and back again. Stiff fingers and sore arms were not conditions that any musician playing for his or her life wanted. But that's how it was, and I frequently chastised myself for forgetting just how fortunate we newly assigned jazz musicians were compared to many others.

Whether we became the minions or maestros of the SS doctor who had recognised me during my time in the infirmary, I never really worked out, but it was through his actions, that a discrete number of us found ourselves pumping out swing rhythms and florid melodies at secretly organised concerts. How bizarre these affairs were, with guards posted on the doors and a strict directive to play as quietly as possible. Pianissimo jazz?

Immense though our efforts were to provide entertainment, the doctor's moods could swing as much as our music did. On the day he gave us the all-clear to be relieved of the more physical work duties in favour of making music, he had we few musicians marched, under armed escort, to an empty barracks some distance from our own. Such was the tortuous route that we took, none of us could quite work out where we were in relation to our own barracks. I need not tell you what we expected our fate to be. Until, once our eyes had become accustomed to the dimly lit space, we could make out a collection of instruments, unlovingly piled up in one corner. I recognised them immediately. Among them was a guitar, a piano accordion, and a double bass. This could only mean one thing. Here lay, what had become, instruments of death. Instruments which once played a merry tune, but which were unwittingly complicit in the deaths of an entire Romani family.

How I managed to prevent myself from, in the first instance, being physically sick, and, in the second instance, from tearing the head off the shoulders of the guard who was closest to me, I cannot say. In any case, my stomach was too empty to spare any of its contents and I was far too feeble to carry out an assault. Needless to say, the pitiful sight left a bitter taste in my mouth, and a deep sense of shame that my body had succumbed so, to the deleterious lifestyle that had left me utterly incapable of striking a blow on behalf of those men, women, and children.

Either the doctor had the sickest sense of humour imaginable, or he had become completely desensitised by the daily horrors he witnessed, and from the influences of his fellow officers. Whichever it was, just what drove him to act in this way was totally beyond my understanding.

As one gets older, I suppose it is only natural to start to question the reliability of your memory. A person can begin to wonder, when they re-visit the canvasses of their past, whether he or she begins to see them in faded or different colours. I'm not sure. Over the years I have perhaps expended too much energy in trying to justify the SS doctor's behaviour, pondering that, surely, he would have signed up to the Hippocratic Oath, swearing to the healing gods to uphold the standards and ethics of his profession.

Decades on from these experiences that I now recount to you dear reader, after I had settled in Tel Aviv, I was visiting a library searching for a text in the music section. Someone must have mistakenly returned a volume to the wrong shelf and quite by chance, I came across a book on Hippocratic writings. Something in me prompted me to open it. I nonchalantly thumbed through some of the pages, taking little notice until one particular page seemed to open up before me, as if of its own volition. I suspect someone must have opened a door somewhere, and a wisp of air had turned into the page-turning fairy. The page revealed a most illuminating piece of text.

In the days of Hippocrates, establishing yourself as a physician would have depended less on how you had been trained, and more on reputation acquired in practice. Whereas the question of a doctor's competence could therefore be disputed, he nevertheless faced the formidable problem of winning the confidence of his clients and of maintaining that confidence. I took a little time to digest this, and in the privacy of the library shelving, was able to express my gratitude to the page-turning fairy by reading on a little further. Questions came back into my mind regarding the SS doctor. I speculated. Did he use his powers to help the sick to the best of his ability and judgement? Did he abstain from harming or wronging man in the way he used his powers? Please excuse my somewhat inappropriate or perhaps insensitive turn of phrase, when I make the suggestion that the doctor was, selective.

It is staggering, is it not, that included in the Oath, is the dictate stating that a physician will not give a fatal draught to anyone if asked, and furthermore, that he will not suggest such a thing? I shall say no more on this topic, other than to share with you that I did eventually manage to thread some thoughts together to try and explain the doctor's motives for what he did. I supposed that despite his training, he was indeed faced with the formidable problem of winning and maintaining the confidence of his superiors. To them, he had to display inhumanity for the sake of his survival. As I have already made known to you, he did take a considerable risk when he first arranged for me to meet with Rose. And he was also promoting forbidden music.

Certainly, the circumstances surrounding the eventual coming together of the secret jazz ensemble require some detangling to be fully understood, but I suspect a full understanding will never be established. But play we did, for the entertainment of the SS doctor and his jazz loving intimates. As far as we were concerned, the instruments we played contained Romani DNA, and we treated them as such, with high respect and reverence. When we saw the expressions of delight on the many faces of those we entertained, we few would share a secretive look, so quickly executed, that the SS officers were certain not to notice it. It was our silent language with which we communicated as we played. With this look, we reminded ourselves in a way which was imperceptible to our audience, that the music we made was not for their pleasure, nor was it to raise their spirits, but to raise the spirits of that lost Romani family. Through our playing, they did rise up and we saw them dance.

'…don't you see, this wind in the trees
is like a musical note.'

Chapter 15

The Lost and The Found

As I have already made known to you dear reader, during that time when I first lost my love for the violin, had it been a living breathing family member, I would have refused to recognise them. But now I say this; if music were a person, it would be the bravest person alive, and I would be glad to know them. Why? Because music can go anywhere unhindered once it springs from the strings, or bounces from a tensioned surface, or rises in the air from a pair of human bellows. Fences, fear, and foreboding become harmless vapour in its presence. The faintest flap of a bird's wing can disperse such things. Music wags a reproachful finger at adversity, in motion like a metronome set at an indefatigable pace that cannot be held back or stopped. Did we find music? Was it our efforts that befriended us to this formidable form of expression? Or did music find us? Did music look into our futures, and on seeing the bleak horizon, decide to offer us protection from the approaching storm? Dear reader, this is not hyperbole. It is the way a grateful man, who is documenting a part of his past, feels about music, for without it, he would surely never have been able to write these recollections. He would have been dust long, long ago.

Music kept us alive. I wish I could say this for all of us. We could not have predicted when an end to this life of cruel confinement would come, or whether it would come at all. We had learnt to interpret freedom in a number of ways; being murdered or getting sick was among them. Noach was the first of us to experience release from his sufferings. I remember it vividly. The guards, for reasons unknown to us at the time, seemed particularly keen to escort us to our rehearsal barracks. It appeared that Noach had somehow got there ahead of everybody else. We found his lifeless body slumped in a chair. The SS guards had hung a sign around his neck. It said, 'I tried to escape.'

This was the last time we ever had to play for our secret SS audience. Our soundscape then became very different. It was the Spring of 1945, and the shouts of the guards, and the collective trudge of thousands of force-marched feet, gradually faded from our ears, as line upon line of detainees headed westward to other camps still within German territory. The Germans had known for some time that the camp would eventually have to be abandoned. Opposing forces were advancing. When the time came, detainees were put to work destroying the evidence of their despicable treatment. Then decisions had to be made as to who would march, who would be put to death, and who would be left behind? Musicians? Would they march? Despite the pleasure that we had provided at those secret concerts, we knew that we were not indispensable, and remember, conditions for prisoners were so bad, that even with the benefit of slightly better food and clothing, maintaining any degree of strength or health was a fearsome challenge. And so, we remained at the camp. If the SS doctor had been playing any kind of game with us, he had the final say, as to whether or not we would ever leave. We, that had been left behind to fend for ourselves, knew that many would die on that march, if not from the cold, then from the bullet. Had we the physical capacity, we could easily have followed them long after they had disappeared from our view, and without getting lost. A trail of corpses lined the route.

Gone were the barking dogs, the piercing shrills of the whistle, the crack of gunfire and the cries of pain and fear. For reasons beyond number, during our time in this place, we had felt abandoned. We had certainly been abandoned now. We were in our hundreds, but can you imagine how alone we felt? We were the weak, the diseased, and the dying. We had no food, no fuel, and no water. The strongest among us tended to the sick. Other than this, there was no movement and no sound. All was silent.

But wait! No! It was not silent. Let me explain. Do you remember, dear reader, my excursion into the woods as a love-struck young boy? I fell into the arms of the woods, and into the hands of the Romani troupe. It was not just their music that had impressed me. It was also their affinity with their surroundings. That is a good word, affinity. They saw things and heard things, out there in the woods, that I had hitherto been blissfully unaware of, the exception being, of course, the sound of the cuckoo. I did, in fact, make further visits to their encampment; that is, until they left, such is their itinerant lifestyle. These Romani people somehow seemed to connect with their environment, but they were not tied to one specific place. They did not enjoy confinement. I remained with my own community, but as part of a jazz quintette I was able to travel. My mother had often reminded me that I was an inquisitive boy. I grew into an inquisitive young man, and those visits to libraries, back in my jazz quintette days with my brother Levi, were not solely dedicated to reading up on

Romani particularities. It is difficult to study a community of travellers without considering the wonders of the natural world; although, I must admit, these extracurricular activities, were as much to impress my younger brother, as they were to satisfy an interest in anthropology and nature. In my studies, I came upon a word. This word was psithurism, the wind in the leaves of the trees. It is a beautiful word.

I suppose you may be thinking, 'Why has Ari digressed so?' But, don't you see, this wind in the trees is like a musical note. It is always there, but seldom heard. Up until that moment, as a detainee, in that Spring of 1945, when the camp had fallen silent, I had understandably not given the forgotten voice of the wind a single thought. But now, the atmosphere was different, and amid this quiet misery, it began to whisper to me. There it was, high in the canopy. I closed my eyes and invited others to join me. Our eyelids sealed out the light and we listened. To us, it was the sweetest music. It was as if all the instruments that had once played and been lost, had, in a united effort, synthesised their best and most inspiring sounds and commissioned the wind to play them. Some said it was a heavenly breeze, sent down from the lips of the Almighty. Others said that Mother Nature was blowing a tender kiss.

Whatever it was, it came down from above and flitted among us. I imagined it sweeping up the ashes of the dead unto heaven. In our emaciated state, we must have fallen asleep to nature's lullaby. For how long, I do not know. When we opened our eyes, before us stood rows of uniformed men with rifles. Their bodies were motionless, and their eyes equally fixed on ours. They were Soviet troops. They said they had come to liberate us.

You could tell, by their faces, that they had no idea that Auschwitz existed. In that moment we wondered whether the Soviet soldiers existed. Had we really awoken from our sleep, or had slumberland also enslaved us, only to add further confusion to our tormented minds with an illusion. Had we not dreamed enough about freedom during every waking hour? As our sleepiness evaporated, and the reality of our awakening materialised, the disbelieving soldiers stood and looked. It was like a reversed roll call, and we subjugated spirits were inspecting the lines. But we were not looking for signs of weakness as the SS guards did; we were looking for signs of compassion. It was there, in the reddening eyes of the Red Army soldiers. It was there in abundance.

Euphoria cannot be suppressed by frailty of the body, nor by the sluggishness of the mind, and although only inwardly expressed, we had euphoria in abundance on that day. A new day had at last dawned.

With confidence, I can report to you that Rose did succeed in her mission to improve conditions for the women's orchestra, and to create something positive out of the destruction. Furthermore, during her time as their leader, not a single life was lost; that is to say, none of her musicians were ever selected. Only three did not live to see the end of the war that was to come some seven months later. One of them was Rose.

'...if we all took the time to listen to what music
has the potential to say to us, then we would
understand one another much better.'

Chapter 16

A Timely Excursion

I hope you will forgive me for omitting from my account any further details about Rose. As with my parents, the best I can do is to leave her in peace, and so I shall say no more on the subject. No more.

But, dear reader, I have not forgotten you. I am not leaving you just yet. There is still some life in me, and as you will soon read, I still have an enquiring mind. And thank you for being my companion throughout these recollections and meanderings. I should not have wanted to make this journey without you. I am used to being alone, but what gets me through is always believing that someone else is there, right next to me.

There is a theory. A linguistic theory. It has been termed, the Sapir-Whorf hypothesis. I hope I am impressing you. Although now out of favour, it was popular in the 1930s. It postulated that the language we speak influences the way we think; that people of different languages perceive the world differently. With this hypothesis in mind, let me explore things a little further. If

German Jews spoke German as their native tongue, which of course a great many did, and if this hypothesis were to be true, then surely, it would follow that the German Jews and the native Germans would perceive the world in the same way. Clearly, my friend, this did not happen during the period in world history in which I set my narrative.

There was a time, in those first few years after Liberation when I began to piece my life back together, that I would have held personal and very firm views about the world and its people. I would have looked at you and asked,

'Is there any shore, lapped by the waters of the seven seas, which has not witnessed scenes of abject cruelty? If you know of any, tell me, and I shall go and live there.'

As my time with you begins to approach its close, I should like to offer you a more optimistic perspective. I would put it to you that, whatever your origins or mother tongue, if we all took the time to listen to what music has the potential to say to us, then we would understand one another much better. We would make allowances for our differences, and my belief is that discord would find a resting place; a place where it could become like the forgotten whisper that would return to us, in our time of need with renewed understanding. Something to ponder.

"Can you tell me one thing,
just how do you carry on?
When everything you ever loved is stolen,
lost or gone
Bitterness, the sweetest cup, let's drink it,
then we're through
For there's nothing we can change here,
nothing we can do."

'I was shaking as I opened the protective coverings
in the shape of a small rectangular crate.'

Chapter 17

My Workshop and its New Residents

My reader friend, timely intervals are periodically required in circumstances where concentration has been focused, and the body in postural fixation, such as when attending a concert or indeed, spending time reading a book. The author of such works should not be forgotten and relief from their efforts must be allowed, if not to fill the belly, and quench the thirst, then for other essential reasons. You see, I am at that age when, shall we say, certain bodily functions have to be attended to rather more often than they did in my youth. But here I am, back again, settled and seated. It was fortunate that I returned to my workshop when I did. I was just in time to answer the telephone. It was an enquiry from the National Music Museum, University of Dakota, asking how things were progressing with the restoration of the priceless Amati violin. Naturally, I reminded them that restorations can take a good deal of time. Such things cannot be rushed. They were satisfied when I assured them that the violin would be ready within the time agreed.

Oh, the thrill I felt on that day when the instrument finally arrived at my workshop. I even gave the place a good clean in preparation, and if I could have afforded it, I should have hired a string quartet to welcome it through the door. I was shaking as I opened the protective coverings in the shape of a small rectangular crate. I lifted the contents like a new-born out of its cradle. After a few careful clicks of catches, there it was, in my arms receiving my affection. Of course, I apologised to the other instruments who daily received my veneration, and I reassured them that I still thought of them as my family, and that I loved them just as much.

My instructions were to confirm the authenticity of the instrument, and after a detailed assessment of its condition, to restore it to its former glory. I have found that with such a complex and intricate task, there is no better place to start than with reading the label. The responsibility of determining correctness of attribution is not to be taken lightly. It is well known among the violin making world that labels are unreliable in identifying an instrument's maker, age, and place of origin. Labels should, as a rule, never be believed. It was, remember, compulsory labelling, in the form of a yellow badge, that was supposed to identify Jews as religious or ethnic outsiders.

The skilled construction of the violin, was more or less, perfected in the eighteenth century, and ever since then, later makers have tended to copy the early master-crafted instruments. A perfect copy, with a convincing label, can deceive the untrained eye. It is true that two different instruments may perform equally well, but it is the one with the famous name attached to it that will command the higher price on the market. Not forgetting, of course, that some violins will be valuable antiques. But this fact interests me little. I am more concerned with their other qualities.

Despite my own views and sentiments, I had my brief to fulfil, and to that end I called upon all my resources and expertise in authenticating the Amati. The label is usually inside the left-hand f-hole, the bass side, and invariably a thin carpet of dust presents the first challenge for identification once under a well-directed examining light. Knowing a little Latin and Italian helps, but there is no substitute for meticulous observations. I noted the shape of the arching, the purfling and the quality and hue of the varnish. I studied these things with my accustomed fastidiousness, and at a pace that the swinging pendulum of an old grandfather clock would have no difficulty in keeping up with.

And then, my attention turned to focus on the instrument's beautifully carved neck. I rotated it to examine the fingerboard, and as my eyes followed its line upwards, I noticed an almost imperceptible indentation at the junction between the pegbox and the scroll. I looked, I paused, and then I stopped my breath, and had to blink in an effort to refocus my eyes and look again. I looked long and hard at this unmistakable anomaly. Now I was sure beyond any shadow of a doubt, that this instrument was indeed an Amati. Yes, it was an Amati. The very same that I had given to my dear brother Levi over forty years ago.

I had to turn off the inspection light. No amount of light could have helped me to see through my liquid-filled eyes. Saltwater is not kind to the carefully varnished surface of a violin, as members of any gate orchestra will tell you, so I tried to pull myself together a little and returned the instrument to its well-travelled case. My tools had been carefully laid out in preparation for any work that needed to be carried out, but I could not pick them up. Without a steady hand and clear vision, it would have been foolish to even touch the Amati. All my shaking hands could do was to reach for the telephone. I needed to make a long-distance call. Could the University tell me anything about my brother? In that one letter my brother had sent to me, he said that selling the Amati had saved his life. It transpired that the man who had bought it so many years ago had later discovered its true value and tried to find Levi so that he could recompense him. His search proved to be fruitless. But what the man had unwittingly done weighed heavily on his conscience and so he decided to donate the instrument to the National Music Museum. Yes, I was able to prove that the instrument was genuine, but I never found out whether it really had saved my brother's life.

'It was plucked out from the pile of bricks
and timbers that tried to hide it…'

Chapter 18

Out of the Ashes

The hands of the clock, safely housed within the tower in the square adjacent to my workshop, have rotated a great many times since I last added to my story. I began my writings, by introducing them as recollections, a personal account concerning the power of music. In order to achieve this, I had to share with you certain events, which have played a significant part in shaping my life. Did I just use the term significant? They were monumental. The magnitude of those times of turmoil somewhat recedes when I am kept busy. This is a good thing. I am in a better place when I am occupied. I am sure you will understand this, and thus forgive me for neglecting my writing duties. A Luthier must earn a living, like any other who wants to satisfy those basic needs of food and shelter, and, not forgetting in my case, the purchase of selected woods and other materials for the purposes of violin restoration.

The salty stains that appeared on my bench many days ago are still there, but less obvious.

I haven't got the heart to completely remove them. I have come round to thinking that tears may be a good thing, but I must be careful, for I have been saving mine.

The result of my industry means I can tell you that the Amati has been completely restored and is in radiant readiness for the laterally flexed chin and nimble fingers of the virtuoso. I shall be sad to let it go, but then in life, this is what you sometimes have to do. It will be like re-living that moment when, at the port of Cuxhaven, I handed the instrument over to my brother as he was boarding the steamship bound for America. He had hinted that I was mad to hand over the Amati to him, and I had to threaten to throw it into the Elbe River before he would take it. Perhaps I am mad now, to allow it once again to slip away from me. But if Levi is still alive, and still in America, then that is where the Amati should be. It now enjoys the perfectly matching contours of its lined case, waiting for its extra shell of protection before it wings its way back across the waters. I hope it brings joy to all the people who will, no doubt, pay it a visit back in Dakota. The museum has had strict instructions from myself that, under no circumstances, must the Amati be sentenced to a life in the confines of a glass viewing case. 'By all means let it be seen,' I told them, 'and by as many people as possible. But above all, let it be played.'

I apologise if this most recent entry has dampened any of your expectations that the restored Amati was being prepared for a grand concert, complete with all the glitter and pomp that often accompanies celebrities. No, my friend. Not on this occasion. I can, nonetheless, satisfy your expected curiosity, by telling you that something rather special is about to happen at this juncture. An adventure, after all, deserves a fitting finish. Right now, I wish you could see my workshop. Do your best, if you will, to bring it into your mind's eye. See the walls with their rows of instruments, all situated a safe distance from the light of my dusty windows, and see the racks which hold the precious woods, and the cabinets and drawers which act as the living quarters for an array of specialised tools. Now see my workbench, and on it, a most prized possession. Yes, that's right, it is a violin. See me holding it for you. Look at it and wonder to yourself, where it must have come from. Another music museum perhaps?

This instrument was rescued from the rubble produced by the destruction of some of the buildings in Auschwitz, when the SS officers tried to erase evidence of their atrocities before they forced marched thousands on a deadly course, westwards. It was plucked out from the pile of bricks and timbers that tried to hide it, by a Soviet soldier. Whether he was a musician or not I cannot say, but he reached for it, and it was saved. I suspect he was a musician. You see, it was obvious that the instrument would be impossible to play due to its condition, but this soldier still thought it was worth something. I do not know the details of how, in its unplayable state, it was kept from being discarded. Perhaps the soldier put it away somewhere and forgot all about it, or perhaps he deliberately preserved its appearance, as a reminder of the circumstances in which it was found. If the latter was the case, then it was a noble thing to do. But it is enough for you to know that it eventually came into my possession. In my long Luthier life, I have acquired a reputation as the rejuvenator of abused, unused, and damaged instruments of antiquity, and, periodically, such instruments are, to my personal joy, delivered to my door.

As I did with the Amati, I gave the rescued instrument my full attention and inspected it thoroughly. I could tell immediately from its condition that it had been played out in the elements. When I made my customary search for a maker's label, it was impossible to read. The body of the instrument was filled with black powder. When I discovered this, I think even the clock in the square momentarily stopped, as if missing a heartbeat. I knew what this powder was. It was ash that had once fallen like dark snow from the tall chimneys of the crematoria, signalling the disposal of human remains. It was of little consequence that I could not read the label. I knew at once, that this violin had belonged to my good friend Noach. If ever an instrument deserved to be played again, it was this one, and I was determined to do everything in my power to make it so.

Look around again in your mind's eye if you can. See the living wood which decorates the walls of my workshop. To me, these instruments really are my family. My only family. They can tell their own stories. Once broken, they are now mended and beautiful once more. Can you see them? Can you hear them? Do you play? If you do, I truly hope that whatever instrument you have chosen, it will be an instrument of peace.

Ari Vander.

'...*an instrument of peace.*'

Acknowledgement

The storyteller featured in this book is an invented character, as are the various other characters he describes and interacts with. However, because the story is underpinned by actual historical events, the author considers it to be neither fair, nor accurate, to describe the book entirely as a work of fiction. For many, it is almost certain, that the subject matter covered in Ari Vander's story, will have a very real impact.

It is therefore entirely necessary to pay tribute to all peoples who were unjustly and cruelly incarcerated in concentration camps during World War II. Their suffering defies explanation and wrenches at the heartstrings. It is sincerely hoped that this book will play its part in preserving the memory of the innocent victims of the Holocaust.

Bibliography

www.amati.com [Accessed 31-01-21]

www.auschwitz.org [Accessed 14,15-01-21]

www.aviolin.com [Accessed 31-01-21]

www.britannica.com [Accessed 15-01-21]

www.cmuse.org [Accessed 31-01-21]

www.encyclopedia.ushmm.org
[Accessed 13, 15, 16-01-21]

Frederick. R. Limited. 1999. *The 20th Century.
A Reflection. A Fully Illustrated Millennium Souvenir
Showing Important Events and Dates Throughout
The 20th Century*. Robert Frederick Limited. Bath:
p72.

Grymes. J. A. 2014. *Violins of Hope. Violins of the
Holocaust – Instruments of Hope and Liberation in
Mankind's Darkest Hour*. Harper Perennial. New York.

www.history.com [Accessed 13-01-21]

www.holocaust.cz [Accessed 13-01-21]

www.holocaustmatters.org
[Accessed 13-01-21]

www.holocaustmusic.ort.org
[Accessed 20-01-21]

www.holocaust.umd.umich.edu
[Accessed 14-01-21]

Lloyd. G. E. R. 1978. (Ed). *Hippocratic Writings*.
Penguin Books. London: pp 9,15 and 67.

www.mjhnyc.org [Accessed 14-01-21]

www.nlm.nih.gov [Accessed 23-01-21]

www.psychoanalysis.org.il [Accessed 13-01-21]

www.sciencedirect.com [Accessed 23-01-21]

www.solarsystem.nasa.gov
[Accessed 23-01-21]

www.stringsmagazine.com
[Accessed 31-01-21]

www.theatlantic.com [Accessed 23-01-21]

www.theholocaustexplained.org
[Accessed 15-01-21]

www.thoughtco.com [Accessed 24-01-21]

www.voyager.jpl.nasa.gov [Accessed 23-01-21]

www.wisesayings.com [Accessed 14-07-21]

www.yadvashem.org [Accessed 15-01-21]

About the Author

William Varnam recently retired from working as a Back Care Adviser for the NHS. Previous to this, he has worked in industry and social care. Before switching careers, he worked as a freelance performer, earning a living as a storyteller, performance poet, actor, and musician. He received formal training in Theatre Arts at Newark College and studied Community Theatre Arts at Rose Bruford College of Theatre and Performance. Since his 'retirement' William has been immersed in numerous creative collaborations involving music and theatre.

About the Broken Instruments Project

As outlined in the introduction to this book, Broken Instruments has been produced in other formats which include a musical dramatization with original songs, a music album, and an audio version. For more information on the Broken Instruments project, you can visit:

www.brokeninstrumentsthemusical.co.uk